Mia

Lets½Go

Crawdad Beach Series (Book 7)

Lisa Buffaloe

Mia Lets Go

Visit the author's website at https://lisabuffaloe.com.

Cover Design: JoAnn Durgin

ISBN: 978-1-957715-34-6 (eBook)
ISBN: 978-1-957715-35-3 (Paperback)
ISBN: 978-1-957715-36-0 (Hardcover)

Mia Lets Go

Mystery writer Jim Petterson hadn't planned on his line of work. He'd been reasonably content as a college professor, but after his wife left him for another man, he'd been ready for a change. In the middle of the night, the thought just came to him, and ten years ago, he jumped into a new career.

Now, he needed to figure out how to kill someone and make it look like an accident. He'd done this kind of thing many times before but needed new ideas, and his friend, Chester, promised he knew the perfect person to help.

With all Mia Burns had been through over the years, she was lucky her body continued to function. She'd been shot, stabbed, and beaten to a pulp. Being strong came in handy, and her multi-ethnic background allowed her to easily blend into most situations. However, now that she was older, the work that took her around the world was getting more difficult.

Her close friends knew what she'd once done for a living, but she couldn't risk that becoming common knowledge because, in Crawdad Beach, she'd found the home she'd never known. Could she trust God enough to let go of her past and step into her future?

Book 7 of the Crawdad Beach Series.

Table of Contents

Chapter 1

Why did the directions bypass the freeway? Crawdad Beach was on the ocean, wasn't it? Jim Petterson glanced at his GPS as he drove the remote two-lane country road.

Every few miles, blacktop or gravel driveways led to houses or farms. Trees and blooming crepe myrtles sported their vibrant spring colors as he drove on. He crossed a bridge over an inlet waterway with a small sandy river. Maybe he should have asked more questions the last time he talked to his friend.

With a shrug, Jim continued driving. He needed to focus on trying to figure out how to kill someone and make it look like an accident. Sure, he'd done that kind of thing many times, but he needed new ideas, and Chester promised he knew the perfect person to help. They'd met years ago, and with Chester's extensive military background, hopefully, his connections would be just what Jim needed.

He hadn't planned on his line of work. He'd been reasonably content as a college professor, but when his wife left him for another man, Jim was ready for a change. Ten years ago, in the middle of the night, the thought just came to him, and he'd jumped into a new career. Most people started young. He'd been in his fifties before he had his first hit.

Jim stopped at a blinking red light and stared at a sign with a cartoon crawfish welcoming people to Crawdad Beach. A small gas station with a convenience store stood on one corner. Across the street was a volunteer fire department beside a large white-steepled church.

Continuing the journey, he crossed an unused railroad track. A public library in the old railroad station had a mural painted on the side of a cartoon crawdad sitting on a beach reading a book. Jim groaned. How on earth would someone living in a town with cartoon crawdads be helpful with planning a murder?

He slowed as the blacktop road became a brick-paved street. Neatly maintained, two-story brick buildings lined the road. Jim read the names of the businesses. Besides a law office, post office, and two buildings with loft apartments, the town had Knick Knacks Antique store, Curl and Dye Beauty Salon, Tiddlywinks Restaurant, Rolling in the Dough Bakery, and Doohickeys Hardware Store. He grinned as he read their sign that said since 1916, they proudly offered a wide range of hardware, building supplies, and whatever whatchamacallit needed. What had he gotten himself into?

Jim found an empty parking place and pulled his car in front of the boutique hotel where he had his reservation. He took his laptop and overnight bag out of the trunk and stood on the sidewalk.

Boutique hotels were supposed to be located in fashionable urban locations. Crawdad Beach seemed more along the lines of quirky and homey.

Oh well, he was here, might as well check in and find out if Chester's contact would provide what he needed.

Jim stepped into the lobby onto what looked like original wood flooring. Brick walls and rich wood paneling gave a modern yet old-world feel.

"Welcome to Hotel de Crawdad." An attractive woman with dark brown eyes greeted him as she stood behind a counter. "Will you be staying with us?" Behind the clerk were photos of the building in the early 1920's.

He stepped to the check-in desk and noted her nametag. "Yes, Crystal. My name is Jim Petterson. I have a reservation for one night."

"Mr. Petterson, welcome to Crawdad Beach. Since you checked in online, your room is ready. I also have a message for you." She handed him his card key and a small envelope. "Will you need help with your bags?"

"No, thanks. I'm good."

"You can take the stairs, or the elevator is straight ahead. I hope you enjoy your stay."

"Thanks, Crystal." Jim followed the curved staircase to the second floor. As he entered his room, he noticed a king-sized bed, desk, chair, and bathroom with a claw-foot tub and shower. What stood out to him were the exposed beams, brick walls, and a balcony that overlooked the main street. *Not bad*.

Jim tossed his overnight bag on the bed, set his laptop on the desk, then opened the envelope. Chester had invited him to dinner at his house. Jim checked the time. *Good*. He had until this evening before he met his contact.

Making notes on his computer, Jim pictured Chester's contact as a muscular man with eyes like steel, his mind hardened from years of military service and seeing things no person should ever see.

Her back against the weight bench, Mia Burns groaned as she lifted the weights and finished her set. With a flick of her wrist, the bar clanked and connected to the slot on her Smith Machine. Since she didn't have a spotter, the apparatus with the bar fixed within steel rails kept her safer and her movement more fluid.

She patted the sweat off her face with a towel as she stood. Even at her age, she could still bench press a good amount of weight. With all she'd been through over the years, she was lucky her body continued even to move. She'd been shot, stabbed, beaten to a pulp a few times, and involved in car wrecks after high-speed chases.

Mia ran her hand through her spiky silver hair. Thankfully, her face hadn't suffered damage, and with her mixed-heritage genetics, she still looked twenty years younger than most women her age. Of course, a plastic surgeon had helped tweak a few areas. Yet, no matter how hard she worked out and tried to eat healthy, slight negative changes in her body and strength continued.

If she quit her job, how could she keep herself busy? For

now, she'd keep working. Last week, she'd traveled to Italy and finished her assignment in only twenty-four hours. She probably should have spent time sightseeing after completing her mission, but Crawdad Beach kept drawing her back.

She'd found the home she'd never known in this little town. The only thing that worried her was how the townspeople would treat her if they knew who she'd been in the past.

Chapter 2

Sitting on Chester's family room sofa, Jim leaned forward and kept his voice quiet. "You're sure your contact is willing to talk to me?"

"Of course, I'm sure." Chester, his silver-haired, still-in-great-shape friend, looked at him like he was offended he would even suggest such a thing. "A few years ago, my friend was the best in the business and still is at work around the world. Just last week, Italy called for help."

"I've never met anyone in that line of work before. Is it safe to talk to them?"

"Safe?" Chester scoffed out a breath. "I wouldn't be sure about that, but you should get your questions answered."

Jim swallowed to wet his dry throat as he glanced around the room. On one wall, a row of built-in shelves contained family photos, Chester's numerous military awards and rows of books neatly arranged by height. A large picture window overlooked a neatly trimmed backyard. The kitchen and dining area were to his right.

"Jim," Chester's wife, Maybelline, with her ever-present bouffant hairdo, called from the kitchen area. "Can I get you a drink? I have soda, water, or tea."

"Water will be fine."

Maybelline grinned his way. "Don't believe Chester when he says you'll be safe."

Jim gulped and turned his attention back to his friend. "So, how do you know this guy?"

Chester's expression took a mischievous turn that made Jim squirm. "I've known my contact since my early days in the military."

Maybelline gave Chester a sly glance as she handed Jim a glass of water. "Chester still has nightmares about their first meeting."

"I do not. I stopped having them last month." He muttered.

Maybelline chuckled as she walked back to the kitchen.

Jim chugged his ice water. Maybe it wasn't such a good idea to meet someone called the Eliminator. He finished his cold drink, and sweat still trickled down the back of his shoulder blades.

Instead of meeting someone face-to-face, he should have continued looking online for information. He was probably on every government watch list by now, anyway.

Mia sighed as she stood outside Chester's door. She should have said no when he called earlier, but she'd given in when he bribed her with the promise of Maybelline's incredible cooking. Mia groaned. Why had she ever agreed to talk to Chester's friend?

Mia took a deep breath, let it out slowly, then rang the bell.

After a few minutes, the door opened, and Maybelline hugged her. "Oh, it's good to see you."

Surprised at the affection, Mia gave her a quick pat.

"Come on, let me introduce you to our guest." Maybelline led her into the family room.

Chester gave her a polite but wary nod. "Good to see you. This is our friend, Jim Petterson."

Mia tilted her head as she surveyed the man. Where had she seen him? He looked very familiar. He stood six feet tall, with black and silver hair and hazel inquisitive eyes. Nice looking.

"*This* is your contact?" Jim's gaze moved to Chester and Maybelline and then back to Mia. Straightening, he held out his hand. "Nice to meet you."

She shook it. His handshake was nice and firm. "Likewise. I think I've met you before."

His eyebrows raised. "I don't believe so. I'd remember you." He cleared his throat as he stepped back. He bumped into the couch and fell with a plop onto the cushions.

Why was he so nervous?

Mia shot a glare at Chester. "So, just what have you told Jim about me?"

Chester gave a nervous chuckle. "Not too much. Just that you would be able to answer his questions."

"What kind of questions?"

Chester shuffled his feet. "You know. Planning a murder,

stuff like that?"

"Murder?" Mia tempered her voice. "What are you thinking?"

"He wasn't," Maybelline said with a head shake. "I didn't know what he was up to." She stepped next to her husband and wagged her finger in his face. "Chester Taylor, you are a problem."

"True, but you love me and my problems." He nuzzled his wife's neck.

Maybelline's face flamed red. "Stop that right now." She squirmed away from him but grinned. "We have company." She turned her gaze to Mia. "I'm so sorry. I had no idea what he was up to. I just thought he invited you to dinner to meet Jim."

"I did want her to meet him," Chester said. "Jim needs help, and Mia is a helper."

Mia crossed her arms. "What kind of help?"

Chester winced. "Jim just wants to pick your brain about planning the perfect murder."

Mia glared at Chester and then shot a look at his guest with enough force to fry his brain.

Chapter 3

He wasn't afraid of many things, but the gorgeous woman zapping him with her laser beam gray eyes made him wish he could run out the door and never return. Jim tried not to whimper. "It's not real."

Mia stepped closer, her movements catlike. "What's not real?"

"I don't really want to kill someone."

Mia growled. "You just want to plan a murder?"

"Yes." He held up his hand. "I mean, no. Yes, I want to plan a murder, but only on paper."

Her eyes narrowed into slits. "Are you planning this for someone else?"

"Yes and no. I want to write it down to share with other people."

"What?" She looked even angrier.

Jim thought about picking up the sofa cushion and using it as a shield. "I'm a writer!" He didn't mean to yell, but she was amazingly, beautifully scary. Oh, man, he was thinking in adverbs.

Mia ran a hand through her very cool, spiky silver hair. "You're an author?"

"Yes." He nodded and kept nodding. "I'm a mystery

writer, and I needed some new material, and Chester thought you would be willing to help me with some ideas for my next novel." He couldn't breathe.

Mia snapped her fingers. "That's where I've seen you."

"You've seen me?" Good grief. His voice squeaked.

"I've read all your books."

"*You* read my work? I mean, you have? You know I'm not the famous writer with a similar name, right?"

"I know who you are. You're pretty good. You do miss some finer details, but you tell a good story."

At her beautiful grin and the compliment, he felt a little lightheaded. "I do?" Jim gave himself a mental shake. He needed to act like a man. He'd been on the best-seller list and needed to act like it. Getting to his feet, he stood in front of her. "Thank you for the compliment."

Standing so close to the attractive author, she gave a quick nod. "My pleasure." She wasn't a huge fan of his work, but she was a big fan. Okay, she was a touch obsessed. Not like that old television show with the writer and the cop, no it was different. Kind of.

"I hope you're both hungry because I made plenty." Maybelline herded them into the dining room.

Jim held out Mia's chair, waited until she settled, then took his place across from her.

Chester led them in a prayer, then passed the food as fast

as he could. Even though he'd been a commanding officer and they'd known one another for years, he was still nervous around her. Maybe she should go easy on him, but she did enjoy watching him squirm.

As they ate, Maybelline kept the conversation moving as she talked about Crawdad Beach and the sweet people who lived in town.

Mia's peripheral vision was what the eye doctor had termed outstanding. She didn't have to look in Jim's direction to know he was watching her. Even Chester kept sending nervous glances her way.

She wanted to grab Chester by his collar and yank him into another room to find out what he'd told Jim about her profession because even Chester didn't know the rumors about what she did for a living were far from reality. However, her nickname did come in handy.

Mia turned her attention to Jim. "Your last novel was set in Bermuda. Do you travel there often?"

He squirmed in his seat. "No, I just look online for ideas."

That was surprising since his stories were accurate in their descriptions. "What about your other books? Have you been to those areas you wrote about?"

Jim's face reddened as he shrugged. "Well, not exactly. I research online or use travel books, magazines, friends, or other avenues."

She wanted to laugh, but looking at his expression would probably make him even more nervous. "You've done a good job with your stories. I would have thought you traveled often."

"Mia is a world traveler," Chester said as he glanced at her.

"Where's your favorite place?" Jim asked.

"I enjoy the islands and sitting by the ocean, but being here in this little town has been a blessing."

"A blessing?"

Mia considered his question. "Since you are an author who writes what is termed Christian fiction, I'm assuming you are curious about the state of my soul. If that is correct, let me put you at ease. I am a believer and follower of Jesus Christ."

Jim's eyebrows raised. "You can do that in your profession?"

She took a deep breath and released it slowly. "Yes, I can. Certain people have made assumptions about what I do for a living." Mia shot a glare at Chester before returning her gaze to Jim. "Perhaps, after we finish our meal, I can explain. But, you must all swear never to reveal what I tell you."

Chapter 4

Jim settled on the couch, unsure whether to take notes on his laptop or just sit and listen. Arms propped on his legs, he leaned forward. He couldn't believe he had an opportunity to meet, much less talk to, a real live spy and assassin. He didn't want to miss anything she said.

As though in the military, Mia, her hands behind her back, stood in front of them. "I gather you have heard that I'm called the Eliminator."

Jim gave a nervous nod. Chester and Maybelline also nodded.

A slight grin played on Mia's lips. "I have not clarified that misnomer. I have certain skills and am involved in activities that help eliminate . . . problems. However, the methods used do not entail extermination."

"Wait." Chester held up his hand. "I thought you were a, uh, an, you know, an..."

"Assassin?"

"Maybe." He mumbled.

Mia sighed as emotions flickered across her face. "My past and current involvement in military operations is classified. Once I became a Christian, I refused to go on certain missions and retired from the military. I now mainly freelance my services. My goals are to bring criminals to justice, rescue those in trouble, and provide support and protection. If there isn't a way to take care of a situation without deadly force, I'm not going to take that job. You would be surprised at the many tools that can be utilized to remove a threat without the need for total elimination."

Maybelline wiped away a tear. "I'm so glad to hear this. I've been praying for you for years."

"Thank you." Mia's eyes gentled as she looked at Maybelline. "I appreciate that since you probably had a different idea of what I was doing."

"Oh, I did. My imagination was rather fertile." Maybelline shot a look at Chester. "Thanks to someone we know."

Chester squirmed under his wife's scrutiny. "Now, honey, don't look at me like that. I had good intel on our friend."

One of Mia's eyebrows raised. "The intelligence you were given was, let's say, highly exaggerated."

"Now, wait a minute. Top-secret clearance should have given me everything I needed to know."

"True, but you know information is sometimes manipulated to achieve the preferred goals. I am not an assassin, hired killer, or involved in any activities with taking someone's life. However, there are those who prefer that false information remains."

"But why?" Jim asked. "What good does that do?"

Mia's gaze warmed as she turned to him. "That often works in my favor. When you heard you would meet someone called the Eliminator, I'm sure you didn't expect me, did you?"

"No," Jim said. "Definitely not. Never in a million years." Heat rocketed up his back as he stared at the attractive woman.

"Good." Mia grinned. "So, when I'm called on a mission, I'm probably not what they expect either, which makes my job much easier."

"Well, I'll be," Chester said. "All these years, I thought you were one of our nation's finest, you know..."

"Oh, don't get me wrong, I still have my skills." Mia's eyes narrowed, and she took a step toward him. "And I know where you live."

"You're just joshing me." Chester gave a nervous chuckle. "Right?"

Mia hiked her shoulder. "Maybe." She turned toward Jim. "So, how can I be of service?"

Jim had to stifle his own nervous chuckle since most of his thoughts disappeared, which, for a writer, was a significant problem.

Mia sat next to Jim and waited for his response.

A tiny sheen of sweat glistened on his forehead. "I'm sorry, I'm still trying to process what you shared."

"No worries. Take your time." Mia didn't mind at all. At least he smelled good, and perhaps she would have the opportunity to get to know him better. She'd cyber-stalked him for years and knew he was divorced, didn't have children, and lived in Raleigh, North Carolina. His books had often given her a way to escape reality.

Maybelline stood. "Well, while you visit, I will clean the kitchen. Just let me know if you need anything."

Mia glanced her way. "Do you need any help?"

"No, it's fine. You two do what you need to do," Maybelline said with a grin.

"I'll give you a hand." Chester hurried after his wife.

Mia waited until they left the room and turned to Jim. "Where do you get your story ideas?"

"Various places," Jim said. "Sometimes, a news story will spark an idea. Other times, I'll have a thought in the middle of the night. Or, I'll get an idea after praying or reading the Bible."

She studied him. Now, it made even more sense why she liked reading his novels. "That's interesting. I would never have thought that." His storylines were always compelling, leaving her with the satisfaction of a great mystery and yet gently threaded with God's hope.

"God is the master Creator," Jim continued, "and writing novels allows creating a fictional world where my characters can discover more about God or find ways to deal with a problem with God's help."

"Is that why your books don't contain profanity or graphic violence?"

"That's part of the reason. There's enough evil in the world. I don't need to add to it, plus I want to honor God with my writing. So, even when murder is involved in my novels, I don't give too much detail."

"That's one of the things I like about your stories. You draw me in and keep me interested. Did you base the detective in your novels after someone you know?"

Jim hiked a shoulder. "To be honest, Detective Larson is who I'd like to be. He's brave, strong, highly intelligent, and able to solve any mystery that comes his way."

"Well, since Larson is a figment of your imagination, he's part of you. He's your alter-ego."

His head tilted to the side as though he was processing her statement. "I guess so." He paused, then straightened. "Wait. I'm supposed to be interviewing you, not you interviewing me."

Drat. Mia inwardly groaned. She was enjoying talking about him and his books, not discussing murder.

"Are you okay with me asking a few questions?" Jim's voice was gentle, respectful. "If you're uncomfortable with what I ask, tell me to move on. Okay?"

Maybe she could do this. Help Jim with his fictional story and keep her past hidden in the past.

Chapter 5

Jim couldn't get Mia out of his mind. She'd given him great ideas. Besides helping him with his current manuscript, he had three files with notes for additional stories. Mia had agreed to allow him to call her with any questions he might have as he wrote his novels. Jim often used policemen and detectives to help with his stories, but having Mia would add a new depth to his writing.

He pushed away from his computer, rose from his office desk, and crossed to look out the window at his backyard. He probably should mow the grass. He enjoyed nature, but caring for his lawn was a distraction he didn't need.

A realtor had contacted him last month asking if he was interested in selling his place. The value from when he originally purchased his home had skyrocketed. He'd considered downsizing and even prayed about moving and where he should go. Raleigh was a great city, but he'd lived here all his life, and some areas brought back memories he'd rather forget. Maybe he should look at something else, like a townhouse or an apartment.

Chester and Maybelline had pressured Jim to move to their little town before he left Crawdad Beach. It was a nice place, and they had some good-looking loft apartments. He'd already checked online. Jim stopped his thoughts.

Was he considering moving because of the incredible woman he'd met? Mia was gorgeous and fascinating. He'd never met anyone like her. She was guarded, careful with her words and what she shared, but Mia was like a book he'd only cracked open. He wanted to read the rest of her story.

Jim grabbed his cell and called his realtor.

"Could you please slow down?"

Keeping at a brisk pace, Mia glanced at her best friend, Stella, running behind her. "No. I need to keep moving." Mia had worked out for hours and still couldn't relax.

The trail that followed along the river was the perfect place to unwind. Talking to Jim last night had been interesting. No, it was more than that. She'd been comfortable with him. She hadn't shared too much, but part of her had wanted to tell him more. How could she ever let that happen?

Mia increased her pace. She could *not* let a man get under her skin, and she could never, ever let her heart feel beyond a certain point. All these years, no matter how serious a relationship, she'd kept her heart safely caged behind a steel wall.

However, after talking with Jim for a few hours, her heart wanted to vault over the barricade. She was a highly trained agent who had lived through month-long interrogations at the enemy's hands and never cracked.

And now? Now, she was in worse danger than she'd imagined.

Stella hurried to catch up. "At least tell me what is going on."

"It's nothing."

Stella grabbed Mia's arm. "Stop! I'm older than you, remember."

"You are not helping. Plus, you're not that much older." Mia stood still and stared at her attractive friend.

Stella raised her hands. "How can I help if you won't talk to me? You showed up at my house and told me to come to the park with you. I hadn't planned on running a marathon."

"Fine." Mia pointed to a bench facing the river, waited for her friend to sit, and slid beside her. "I'm in a situation I don't know how to fix."

"Sounds serious." Stella's green eyes held compassion. "Did something go wrong with one of your missions?"

Mia groaned. "No, it's personal."

"Oh." Stella's eyes widened. "How can I help?"

"You can't."

"Why did you want me to come with you if I can't do anything? Do you need my cyber skills?"

"No. I don't know what I need. Maybe it's nothing."

"It's obviously not nothing because something has you freaked out."

Mia swallowed hard. "It's my heart."

"Your heart? You have heart trouble?"

"Yes, it was feeling something." She couldn't let that

happen again. The risks were too deep, too dangerous.

"Oh." Stella gasped. "This is serious. Who is he?"

"Jim Petterson," Mia muttered.

"The author?" Stella asked. "You've read all of his books. What does he have to do with your heart?"

"Chester invited him to town so Jim could pick my brain to help him with one of his novels."

"That's wonderful."

"No, it's not wonderful. I spent hours talking with Jim last night, and then I met him for breakfast this morning at Tiddlywinks before he left town." Mia grabbed her friend's arm. "I like him. Do you realize how dangerous that is for me? I can't feel anything like that. If I don't have my emotions under control, how can I do my job? No one will hire me if they find out I like someone."

"You like me, and you've been okay."

"That's different. We've been friends and buddies for ages."

"But, you've had relationships before. You've been engaged; what six times?"

Mia looked away. "Seven, but who's counting?" Most were because of her assignments, but a few men she had cared about.

"How can you be so worried about Jim if you've only met and talked to him for a few hours? You didn't do anything else, did you?"

"Of course not. But there's something about him. Maybe because I've read all of Jim's books, I felt comfortable enough with him that I felt my guard dropping."

Stella put her hand over her mouth for a moment. "Oh my. That is serious. Do you think Jim likes you too?"

"I don't know," Mia whimpered. "Maybe? But who knows? Maybe he acted interested in me because he wanted information."

"Are you going to see him again?" Stella asked.

"I don't know. He has my number."

Stella gasped again. "You gave him your number? Your *real* number? You don't hardly ever give that out."

"I know. See why I'm worried?"

Her friend stared into the distance for a moment. "Since Chester invited Jim to town. Maybe you could talk to him."

"Are you kidding me? I like Chester, but talking to him about this situation would be crazy. How can I keep him squirming and scared around me?"

Stella nudged her. "Maybe it's time to let people know you're human."

"Not happening. Nope. Nada. Get that thought out of your head."

"You could talk to Wilder." Stella offered.

"Your husband is a great guy, but no. He knows my past. I don't need to saddle him with my worries for the future."

"I don't understand. You've felt things for guys before. I know you've cared for other men and been in love. With Jim, just exactly what are you afraid of?"

Mia shook her head. She wouldn't answer that question. Yes, she'd been in love or thought she was in love.

Mia let out a shuddering breath. She'd given a few pieces of her heart to other men, but never in all her years had she felt comfortable enough with *any* man to share who she really was.

Chapter 6

His friends said he was crazy. Maybe he was. Jim kept his eyes on the road as he switched lanes to prepare for his exit off the interstate. He had prayed for guidance and felt confident about where he was going.

When his house sold in two days, Jim had to make a quick move. The couple buying had paid cash and wanted to take possession as soon as possible.

Packing up his belongings hadn't taken long. He didn't have much to move besides his laptop, books, clothes, and a few personal items. He'd donated his yard equipment and tools to charity and anything else he didn't need. When his wife left, she'd taken most of the furniture. Even though it had been ten years, he'd never replaced what was gone. He didn't entertain, hardly ever dated, and spent most of his time with imaginary characters who didn't care how his house looked.

Jim had called and reserved a two-bedroom loft apartment in Crawdad Beach. He'd have plenty of room based on the floor plan and online photos. He wouldn't need to worry about yard work, and the town park and nature trail would provide any outdoor escape he might want. Most of what he might need would be within walking distance since he'd only be a few doors down from the bakery, restaurant, hardware store, and antique store.

It had been three weeks since he'd seen Mia. They'd talked a few times on the phone, and although she sounded pleasant when he called, she seemed guarded.

Although Chester and Maybelline knew he was coming, Jim hadn't told Mia he was moving to her town. Maybe surprising someone called the Eliminator wasn't his brightest idea, but even if there wasn't hope for friendship or more than friendship with Mia, he still felt Crawdad Beach would be a great place to live.

Her life had settled nicely into her unpredictably predictable routine. Mia had spent one week in Mexico on assignment, then enjoyed three days lazing on the beach. The other days were spent in Paris taking care of a situation for a client.

Back home, she'd gotten up early, lifted weights, ran on the trail by the river, showered, and was now preparing to brief her team member, Valentino, on their next mission.

The twenty-seven-year-old Italian young man with dark hair and dark-brown eyes stood six foot five inches tall and was 225 pounds of solid muscle. Being good friends with Valentino's family for decades, Mia had known him since his birth and loved him like he was her own.

Valentino was a friend she trusted in every aspect of her life. Besides his handsome and distracting good looks, his skills in martial arts had come in handy on many assignments. Most people assumed Valentino was the Eliminator, thus freeing Mia to move about with ease.

Her phone signaled an alert that someone was approaching her house. Mia smiled. Valentino was here. She turned off the security alarm and opened the door.

Wearing jeans and a t-shirt, Valentino walked toward her. "Morning," he said as he stepped inside. "Could you remind me what name you're using in Crawdad Beach again?"

"Mia Burns." She motioned for him to follow her to the office.

"Yes, that is correct. Mia is the guardian of justice, and the Burns surname was because you like putting the burn on those who try to get in your way." He chuckled as he walked down the hall behind her. "Please forgive. I should have remembered. I'm still jet-lagged from our last flight." He collapsed into a chair and stretched his long legs in front of him.

She picked up her file and sat in her desk chair. "I know you didn't get much rest since that stewardess kept flirting with you every few minutes."

Valentino stifled a yawn. "She was pretty but not my type. Way too forward. She wore too much makeup, and her false eyelashes kept getting hung up in her eyebrows as she tried to do that flutter thing some women do." He dramatically blinked a few times. "Do you realize how difficult it is to be a nice guy? I get propositioned by all sorts of people. Just because I stay in shape, I'm looked at like a piece of meat."

Mia couldn't help but chuckle. "I'm sorry. I know it's difficult for you. Your mother is proud of you for not sleeping around."

"You know, Momma is a good woman," Valentino said. "And do not get me wrong, I like women. I *really* like women, but I made mistakes when I was younger, and now I must do the right thing. God is watching."

Mia knew that fact all too well. Thankfully, God had graciously forgiven her and turned her life around.

"That's why I like working with you," Valentino said. "Our missions are non-lethal, and we help people. Plus, I get to work with the Eliminator." Valentino cocked an eyebrow and grinned.

"Someday, you might have to take over for me."

"What?" He straightened. "Are you thinking about retiring?"

"Maybe. I don't know. I'm not getting any younger." Mia couldn't believe she voiced that thought, maybe because she'd been praying about what was next for her. But she hadn't even discussed the idea with Stella. Besides that, Mia had no clue what she'd do if she stepped away from her work. The Eliminator was her identity, who she was. But lately, it took her longer to recover and the missions weren't as easy or fun as they had once been.

Valentino leaned toward her, his gaze intense. "What would you do if you retired?"

"I don't know. That's the problem."

"Have you talked to Stella or Wilder? They might have a

few ideas."

Mia nodded. "True, they might." Since Stella was a retired cyber-security spy and her husband, Widler, had sold his security company, they seemed content in Crawdad Beach and stayed as busy as they wanted. Maybe Mia could do the same.

"You could come back to Italy with me, live with my family."

"That is very kind of you. I treasure your family, but Crawdad Beach has become my home."

"I am surprised. I thought you enjoyed living in a large city. Wait, are you still planning on our next mission?"

"Yes. The young woman needs us." Mia spread her file documents and photos across the top of her desk.

Valentino stood next to her and studied the information. "I see why the client did not use the police. Too many complications with this one."

"I agree. I've left messages with my friends in law enforcement in that area to let them know what we'll be doing while in town. I don't ever want to step over the boundaries of other agencies. I'll purchase our plane tickets to Los Angeles once I hear back. I appreciate you agreeing to stay in town for a few days until we're ready."

"It's no problem. The new hotel is nice. I checked in before I came here."

"Why don't we get some lunch at the restaurant, then come back and discuss logistics?"

"Sounds very good. I am looking forward to tasting South

Carolina cuisine."

"Well, I'd be more prepared to try some good hometown southern cooking. We can walk over since it's only a few blocks from the house." Mia locked up, set her alarm, and strolled down the quiet streets beside her friend.

Could she step away from the life she'd built and turn her client list over to Valentino? Even though she'd retired from the military, she continued to work. However, the more she thought about and prayed about it, the more she felt led to release her work. And that thought terrified her.

Chapter 7

Jim couldn't believe he'd actually moved. *Why not?* His parents had passed away, he didn't have kids, his siblings lived in other states, his friends stayed busy with their own families, and he mainly talked to his writer buddies online. Jim looked around his apartment and admired the hardwood floors, brick walls, exposed beamed ceilings, the open kitchen, and a fireplace on the back wall. The French doors leading to a balcony overlooking the main street let in plenty of light.

With the two bedrooms, he'd use one as the master and the other as his office. The place looked even better in person. Yes, this would do just fine. He didn't need much to live on. Most of the money he made in book sales was donated to charity or placed in savings.

Jim hurried down the stairs and went through the back door. The moving truck was already backing into position to unload. He'd used a moving company that hired college kids. They helped him pack his belongings and brought a crew that cleaned his house before they left. He'd paid extra to have the movers follow him as soon as they finished from North Carolina. In less than an hour, the young men had everything off the truck and situated in the apartment.

Once finished, Jim thanked the guys for their hard work

and gave each one a generous tip. Wide-eyed, the guys stood there momentarily, then profusely thanked him and shook his hand.

Jim chuckled. He liked being generous when he could, especially to those not afraid of hard work. He'd make sure to leave an excellent online review and contact the company management to let them know he appreciated the outstanding job they'd provided for his move.

Taking his laptop, he sat at the card table where he ate his meals. After he took care of the phone call and left a review for the moving company, Jim glanced around at his sparse furnishings. Maybe it was time to buy new furniture. He'd noticed a big, everything-you-could-ever-need-under-one-roof store on his way here. Perhaps they had something he could get delivered.

Jim opened their website, and sure enough, they carried furnishings. It didn't take him long to choose a couch, coffee table, entertainment stand, and an industrial-looking metal and wood bookshelf. He even found nice-looking bedroom furniture.

His ex-wife would be horrified at him buying online without even looking at the items. The thought made him smile and order new things for his kitchen. Once he found everything he could want, Jim entered his credit card information. His purchases would be shipped to his place by the end of the week. Now, that was his kind of shopping.

Since he had only a few boxes of cereal, a late lunch at the restaurant would be just what he needed. He'd then drive to the local grocery store, and tonight, he'd dine at Chester and Maybelline's house.

Jim mentally patted himself on his back. For his first day in Crawdad Beach, things were going smoother than he ever imagined.

The look from the townspeople at her handsome friend had been priceless. Mia smiled as they stepped inside the restaurant. She'd already taken Valentino through Knick Knacks Antique Store and Doohickeys Hardware.

At a table along the restaurant's back wall, Valentino sat across from her. "This is a great town. I see why you like living here."

"It's funny how life takes you places you never thought you'd go."

"Yes, I didn't think I would have been able to travel the world. Nor, be in a town with cartoon crawdads as a mascot." He held up the menu and pointed to the crustacean wearing a chef's hat.

"Crawdadians are proud of their heritage."

"Hello, Mia," Chester greeted her as he and Maybelline approached their table. "Who's your friend?"

"Valentino Bandoni, meet Chester Taylor and his wife, Maybelline."

Valentino rose to his feet. "Nice to meet you."

Chester raised to his full height and puffed out his chest.

"I can chew nails."

Maybelline playfully punched him. "Hangnails do not count."

Mia laughed. "Seriously? That's what you had to say?"

Valentino blinked a few times and cast a confused glance at her.

"Don't mind Chester. Believe it or not, he used to be a commanding officer in the military, and he *was* tough."

"Thank you, Mia. I appreciate the compliment." Chester turned his attention to Valentino. "Welcome to Crawdad Beach, young man. What brings you to our town?"

Valentino shrugged. "Just passing through."

"He works with me," Mia said with a grin.

"Oh. Then, I won't ask too many questions. Well, you both have a good day."

Maybelline gave her a little wave as she followed Chester out the door.

Valentino returned to his seat. "You have known him for long?"

"We go way back."

"Stella and Wilder live here too, correct?"

"Yes, you'd be surprised by the stories behind the people who are settled in this little town."

The cute, brown-haired waitress, Ursula, placed two glasses of water on their table. "May I take your order?" Her brown eyes settled on Valentino, and she took on the dreamy look most women got when they saw him.

Valentino glanced up at Ursula. His eyes widened, and his grin took almost a goofy turn.

Mia almost fell out of her chair. She'd never seen him look at a woman like that. Ursula was attractive, and even Mia had noticed that the young woman's eyes held an innocent yet playful look.

"I would very much like you to take my order," Valentino said.

Ursula smiled. "You aren't from around here, are you?" Her voice held a level of awe.

"No, I am from Italy."

"Oh, wow. I've always wanted to go there."

"It is a nice place. You should come."

"Well, I don't travel much." Ursula's cheeks tinted pink. "I haven't even been out of the state. Do you travel a lot?"

"Yes, I have been to many places."

"That's really nice," Ursula's voice was breathy as though she couldn't believe she was talking to someone like him.

"My name is Valentino. What is yours?"

"I like your name. I'm Ursula."

"I like yours also."

Enjoying herself, Mia leaned back in her chair. Young love was in the air.

Ursula sighed, then seemed to shake herself. "Oh, I'm so sorry for taking so much of your time. I better take your order."

Valentino laid his hand on her arm. "No, we are not in a hurry."

Ursula gazed at his hand on her arm as though a king had touched her. "That's very kind of you."

Valentino stood and gazed down at her. "I must leave town soon. Perhaps we could see one another when I return?"

Ursula sighed as she looked up at him. "Oh, I would like that very much."

They continued gazing into one another's eyes. Somewhere in the cosmos, music played.

As much as Mia hated to end the lovefest, she did need to get back to her office. She cleared her throat. "I'm sorry to interrupt, but could we place our order?"

Ursula's cheeks flamed red, and even Valentino's neck reddened. From the look on both their faces, Mia figured they had forgotten they were even standing in a restaurant.

"I am so sorry," Ursula readied her pad and pen.

"Not a problem," Mia said with a smile.

After placing their orders, Ursula seemed to float to the back.

Mia glanced at Valentino. "Our assignment shouldn't take too long. Should I book your flight back to our area when we finish?"

Valentino tried to act nonchalant but she could pick up on his body language. The boy was smitten. "Perhaps that would be best. You probably have a few things we need to discuss before I return to Italy."

"Yes, I believe we do." Mia's chuckle caught in her throat when she spotted Jim Petterson walking toward them. What was *he* doing in town?

"Well, hello." Jim stopped and smiled at her, then cast a curious glance toward Valentino.

"Hi, Jim. Are you here visiting Chester?" Mia took a sip of water and tried to hide the fact her heart was beating like crazy.

"Although I will see Chester and Maybelline this evening for dinner, I just moved here."

Mia choked, sputtered, couldn't catch her breath.

Valentino and Jim fought over trying to give her the Heimlich maneuver. Gagging, coughing, and flailing against their bodies, she realized she might die before she'd take another breath.

Chapter 8

Just who was the massive behemoth of a man fighting him while he tried to help Mia? Jim tried to muscle in and help the poor woman. She was choking! "Back away, bucko!" Jim yelled.

The guy shoved him with enough force that Jim flew against the next table. Thank goodness it was empty. Ready to fight, he got to his feet.

"Stop it!" Mia yelled. She coughed and coughed some more. "I'm fine. I just choked on some water." She turned to the other restaurant guests. "Sorry about the excitement."

Mia plopped in her chair. Her gaze bounced back and forth between Jim and Valentino, then she grinned. "You know, I've dreamed of dying in a man's arms. I didn't think it would be because water went down the wrong pipe. Valentino Bandino meet Jim Petterson."

"The author?" Valentino held out his hand. "Sorry about shoving you."

"No worries." Jim shook the man's massive hand. "Yes, I'm a writer. Not that famous guy with a similar name, but I do pretty well."

"I know which one you are. I've read all your books."

"You have?" Jim felt his eyebrows rise.

"Yes," Valentino said. "I use an e-reader when I travel. You tell a good story. You do, however, miss some of the finer details."

"Yeah, I've heard that from someone we both know." Jim cut his eyes toward Mia.

"Would you like to join us for lunch?" Mia asked. "We just ordered."

"If you both don't mind, that'd be great." Jim sat. "So, how do you two know one another?"

"We work together," Mia said.

"Interesting."

A faint smile on her lips, Mia tilted her head as she stared at Jim. "Did you say the words back off, bucko?"

The burn of embarrassment flared up Jim's back. "Maybe," he muttered.

Valentino chuckled. "Those words came from a famous author. Too funny."

Jim did his best to act tougher than he felt. "In my defense, I thought Mia was in trouble, and you weren't helping."

"She will always be safe with me." Valentino's eyes narrowed as he scowled at Jim.

"Okay, guys." Mia's palm shot up, a warning glare in her eyes. "Before you two break into a bucko brawl, why don't we get the waitress to take Jim's order?"

"I will get Ursula." Valentino jumped to his feet and was gone in a flash.

"Who is that guy?" Jim asked.

"He's a good friend and helps in my work," Mia said. "I've known him and his family for years."

"Sorry about earlier. I was only trying to help."

"I appreciate your concern." Mia's voice held a polite but flat tone.

Without Valentino at the table, the conversation wasn't going as Jim had hoped. Why was she being aloof toward him? "I'm sure I couldn't do what Valentino does, but I am loyal to my friends."

One of her eyebrows raised. "Friends?"

"I hope you consider me a friend."

She didn't answer for a moment, just studied him. "So, you moved here?"

Disappointed at Mia's non-answer, Jim tried to keep his shoulders from dropping. "I did. My house sold in two days, so I moved into the downtown loft apartments. Chester and Maybelline have been after me for a while about coming here, and it seems like a great place. Close enough to the ocean and not too far to drive to the mountains." He was rambling. Jim stopped talking.

She continued staring at him as though reading his thoughts. Jim rubbed the back of his neck to ease the tension. Maybe moving here wasn't such a good idea. He'd hoped Mia would be glad to see him. Instead, he felt like an unwanted guest. More than that, she almost seemed hostile to his presence. And from what he knew about Mia, that could be a serious problem.

Valentino returned with the waitress, and Jim placed his

order.

After the young woman left, Valentino turned his attention to Jim. "How do you know Mia?"

"A mutual friend introduced us. Mia has been gracious enough to help me with ideas for my novels."

"That is good. Mia has much to share. You should write her story."

"Mia's story?" Jim took a quick look in her direction. Her focus was on Valentino and if Jim wasn't mistaken, she'd just decapitated him with her laser-beam eyes. "I often use real-life situations or cold-case investigations to spark my ideas, but I've never written non-fiction."

Mia shot her attention at Jim. "We will not discuss that idea further."

Sensing her anger, Jim moved his chair a little further away. What had he done wrong? He'd prayed about coming here, and everything had fallen into place. Everything except what he'd hoped might progress with the beautiful, fascinating woman glaring at him.

Fighting a growl, Mia controlled her breathing. She should never have agreed to help Jim. Why had he moved to Crawdad Beach? Did he plan to use her more often for his stories or hope to get to know her better? Either way, Jim had stepped over the boundaries she'd firmly established in her mind.

She didn't need a man in her life, even if that man did make her heart do a ridiculous skip-type thing as though happy to be around him. Mia fisted her hands in her lap.

How could this be happening to her? She was highly trained to control her body, emotions, and thoughts. The few times she'd allowed someone to cross her protective heart barrier had ended in disaster.

Forget men and forget retirement. She'd take on as many assignments as possible to keep her busy and far away from Jim Petterson.

Chapter 9

"**Do** you think I did something wrong?" Jim placed a slice of roast on his plate and glanced at Chester and Maybelline. He'd already shared with them what happened at lunch.

"Well, I think you stepped over Mia's boundaries," Maybelline said as she passed Jim the mashed potatoes.

"Boundaries?"

Chester gazed for a moment at his wife. "I get it. You think Mia likes Jim but doesn't want to like him?"

"Yes, I think that's what happened," she said.

Jim scoffed. "From the look on Mia's face during lunch, I think she hates my guts."

"Oh, I think that's even more proof," Maybelline grinned.

"I don't understand. Once our meal arrived, Mia hardly spoke at all, other than announcing she planned to be gone for months. Valentino seemed surprised, but she glared at him before he said anything. I think Mia is trying to avoid me as much as possible."

Maybelline pointed her fork at him. "See, I think I'm correct in my hypothesis. She likes you."

Chester glanced at Jim and shrugged. "Woman's logic. It's a tough one to crack. However, Maybelline might have a point. Mia never wants to have anyone get under her skin, and I think you did."

Jim snorted. "Maybe as an annoying irritant."

Maybelline shook her head. "You just met her a few weeks ago, but she's known you for years."

"How can that be?" Had Mia watched him? He sometimes wondered if someone was following him, but that was probably his active imagination since his genre was mystery and suspense.

"You're an author," Maybelline continued. "Besides your books, you have a website, and information about you can be found in articles and social media. Mia is a big fan. Based on her reaction when she first met you and what you shared about your lunch experience, she might have a little crush on you."

"Ha! Now, that's a joke. Isn't it?" Jim glanced back and forth at his friends, who just shrugged. How could Mia like him? He was an ordinary guy with an ordinary life. Wouldn't she be attracted to an international spy or military man? "If Mia likes me, and that makes her hate me, how do I fix that?"

"I don't know that you can," Maybelline said. "Pray and ask for God's guidance and pray for Mia."

"I can do that." Jim took a bite of his meal. If Mia *did* like him, he wouldn't mind having the opportunity to date someone like her. What was he thinking? Situations like that might happen in his novels. Real life was different. His main character got the girl, not him.

"For someone talking about retirement, you have booked a hectic schedule."

Mia ignored Valentino's comment and tried to focus on the novel in her lap. The California mission had been successful, as well as the one in Mexico, and they were now on a flight to Paris.

Valentino knocked her arm off the armrest between them. "I was hoping we could fly back to your town for a few days."

She flipped a page on the novel. "Sorry about that."

"No, you're not." He leaned toward her ear to be heard over the plane's engine noise. "You booked these trips to put distance between you and Jim Petterson."

Mia shot him a look. "I can't help it if our services are needed."

Valentino's eyes narrowed. "You are rushing us into jobs without proper information. You may wish to take risks, but do not drag me into them."

She cringed and shifted in her seat. He was right. "If you want to return to the States, I'll buy you a ticket when we land."

"No, I will continue with you for now." He turned his back on her and closed his eyes.

She deserved Valentino's disdain. Their schedule had more to do with avoiding Crawdad Beach than helping people. Trying to stop her headache, Mia rubbed her forehead.

Something needed to change before someone got hurt, but what?

Detective Larson refused to talk to him. Jim stared at his computer screen. He'd barely written three pages in the last three weeks. How could he write anything when his main character sat in his office staring at the wall?

Jim glared at the blinking cursor, mocking him as though taunting his lack of writing ability. He'd given his character a good life. The least Larson could do was work with him. "Buck up, Detective."

Jim put his head in his hands. Great. Just great. He was talking to his imaginary character. Since Mia had left town, he seemed to have lost his writing skills. Why should her being away even matter? They barely knew one another. Writer's block had never been his problem, but now his mind kept drifting to Mia as he wondered what she was doing and why she was avoiding him.

Usually, his words and stories flowed free. His best sellers were typically based on actual cold case files. Of course, he would change names and locations. Getting to his feet, Jim stretched his back. He needed to buy one of those standing desks because sitting all day made him feel like a marshmallow.

Since meeting Valentino, Jim had developed a rigorous exercise routine. He was in reasonably decent shape, but most of that was from good genetics since his dad had been an athlete. Jim flexed his biceps. Not too bad, but he could do better. Tomorrow, he'd add additional pushups and arm curls to his workouts.

Jim crossed to the French doors and stepped onto his balcony. A warm breeze blew from the coast, and stars shone in the dark midnight sky. Streetlights below cast a soft glow. Stores were closed, and the road was empty except for a few parked cars. The townspeople definitely believed in going to bed early.

He might as well call it a night. Maybe tomorrow, his writing would come together. Pausing, Jim squinted down the street. Was someone standing in the shadows? He shook his head. Probably his imagination.

Surely, nothing would ever happen in a sleepy little town like this. Yawning, Jim went inside and closed the door behind him.

Chapter 10

The gentle sound of the river didn't ease the tightness in Mia's chest. Her running shoes crunched on the gravel as she made a second loop on the trail. Early morning sunshine flitted through the trees, the shade bringing a welcome cooling.

She should be thrilled at their successful missions. Instead, she felt like a failure. Her lack of planning had put Valentino and herself in danger. On the flight home from Paris, Mia had repeatedly thanked God for their protection.

The fast, rhythmic stride of another jogger came from behind. Mia moved to the right to let them pass. A young woman with a lightning bolt shaved in her dark hair smiled in greeting as she left Mia in the dust.

The last few weeks proved it was time to relinquish her business. Her throat constricting, she picked up her pace and ran full speed. How far did she have to run to get away from her regrets?

Last night, she officially relinquished her business to Valentino. It was the right thing to do. Early in her career, a mission had horribly failed because of a lack of preparation from the lead team member. As a result, Andreas, her fiancé, had been killed. Andreas was the one man she'd truly loved. It had taken years for Mia to forgive what happened.

Sweat trickled down Mia's face, and she wiped it away with the back of her hand. Even though she felt like it was the right thing to do, letting go of her business left her feeling stuck in another dimension, unsure of what was next.

Hand in hand, an older couple strolled with a little white dog trotting next to them. Mia said hello as she ran past.

Would she ever have an opportunity to enjoy life with someone? Jim Petterson's face came to mind. Mia groaned. He was the main problem.

She'd been distracted because of Jim. She barely knew the man. Okay, she'd admired him for years and loved his books. Jim's main character solved crimes and brought those who did evil to justice. Even more so, Jim's books always contained a golden thread of a God who heals the brokenhearted, comforts their sorrows, and gives hope for a new beginning.

Mia stopped, leaned over, and placed her hands on her knees as she tried to catch her breath. She needed a new beginning, but what else could she do with her background? She didn't *ever* want to be bored. Money wasn't a problem with her military pension and a decent amount in savings. She'd even paid cash for the house she'd bought from her friend, Stella.

Mia straightened and looked up at the sky. She needed guidance. "God, what do I do now?"

She waited. Nothing happened, no bolt from heaven, nothing came to mind. She couldn't even think of a Bible verse.

A gentle breeze whispered through the trees, and a dove cooed in the branches above. At least it was peaceful.

Mia slowed her stride as she continued on the trail. Two verses popped into her mind. Were those her thoughts, something she'd memorized in the past, or was that her answer? Not sure what to think, Mia picked up her pace and jogged to her friend's house.

"I can't believe you relinquished your business." Stella stared at Mia like she'd gone crazy. "What on earth happened? I thought you'd keep working until you died."

"Yeah, me too." Mia sipped a glass of lemonade while sitting beside Stella on her back deck. She'd already updated her friend on what she'd done.

"Did you think about this, pray about it, or was this some knee-jerk reaction?"

"I did pray about it. I'm not getting any younger. Plus, I was distracted on the last few jobs. If I'm not physically and mentally in top shape, I can't risk putting others in danger."

"I get that, but I'm not sure what to say."

Mia sent her friend a pleading look. "Tell me what I'm supposed to do now."

"That's above my pay grade. I have no idea."

"You're a big help. As hard as this is, I think it's the right thing. But, I do *not* want to sit around and do nothing."

Stella chuckled. "That would be a fate worse than death for you."

"Yes, it would." Mia nodded. "Valentino is staying at the

hotel for a few days. He said he wanted to make sure I had thought things out before he left. He thinks I might change my mind."

"Are you having doubts?"

"No. Maybe?" Mia took a deep breath. "No. I'm sure."

"That sounds decisively indecisive."

"I really do think it's time, but I need guidance. On my way here, I thought of a few verses, but I wonder if that's just me grasping at something I'd read before."

Stella leaned closer. "What were they?"

"The first verse I thought about was trusting the Lord, not relying on my own understanding, acknowledging God, and He would make the path straight. The next one was about waiting for the Lord, being strong, and letting my heart take courage."

"Sounds like you have your answer."

"Just because I thought of a couple of verses?"

"You prayed and asked God for help, and He wants to guide His children."

"I don't know. I do know I need to trust God. That's a given. Without God, I'd never have made it through life. But, maybe I was just remembering what I'd read or heard at church."

"Trusting God is excellent advice. And sometimes, we do have to wait to see what's next on our journey. Waiting isn't just sitting staring at the wall. It's an active focus on God to be ready."

Mia considered the thought. "Like on a mission when we

had to wait for the proper timing to take action?"

"Right," Stella said. "There's another verse that says no eye has seen, nor ear heard, nor the heart of a person even imagined, what God has prepared for those who love Him."

"Well, I can believe that one because I can't see, hear, or imagine what on earth will fill my time."

Hoping to spark his creativity, Jim had spent time at the beach this morning. He hadn't had much luck with writing ideas but did enjoy the time he walked by the ocean. What was strange, while there, he felt like he was being watched.

Jim checked his rear-view mirror as he drove on the interstate back to his apartment. He'd tried to shake off the creepy feeling of being followed, but a black Mercedes C-Class sedan did seem to be staying with him. Jim chuckled. Obviously, he was spending *way* too much time writing mysteries. His concerns had to be only his imagination.

Chapter 11

Unfortunately, this morning's beach walk hadn't given Jim any ideas for his latest manuscript. He pictured Detective Larson shaking his head, disgusted with Jim's lack of progress. He groaned. Non-writers, normal people, would think something was wrong with him for giving imaginary characters life outside the pages of a book.

In his defense, he spent the majority of his day either writing or plotting a story. He even considered Detective Larson's character a good friend. Did that make him strange? Jim shrugged. Maybe it did, but it probably came with the territory of being a fiction writer. Turning on his blinker, Jim switched lanes to exit. Before returning to his apartment, he needed to stop and fill his car with gas.

He exited the freeway and drove into a filling station. As Jim pumped gas into his tank, he stared at the sky. Dark clouds were building on the horizon. If a storm were coming, hopefully, he would have time to get home. The pump clicked off, and Jim took his receipt and returned to the driver's seat.

As he adjusted the rear-view mirror, he noticed the Mercedes parked by the side of the road. The dark-tinted windows concealed the occupant or occupants. The hair on the back of Jim's neck stood in attention.

He *was* being followed. Why? His books sold well, but he probably wasn't famous enough to have a stalker. What would Detective Larson do? Jim buckled in his car. First, he needed to get back on the freeway and make a few moves to verify it wasn't just his imagination about being followed.

He'd taken a defensive driving course a few years ago as research for one of his novels. It looked like that was finally going to come in handy. He acted like nothing was wrong as he drove slowly out of the station. Sure enough, the Mercedes followed.

Jim punched his car's accelerator and merged into the freeway traffic. The black sedan kept a few cars behind. He eased his car into the left lane. Holding tight to the steering wheel, Jim breathed deep, keeping his head clear, enjoying the wonderfully new sensation of adrenaline pumping through his veins.

The exit for the road leading to Crawdad Beach was just ahead. Jim continued driving. If he remembered correctly, the next exit would be the last one for about ten miles after this one. Biding his time, he waited. An eighteen-wheeler traveled to his right. Jim kept at the same speed with the big truck for a few miles.

Seeing his opportunity, Jim stepped on the gas, swerved in front of the truck, then crossed two lanes to hit the exit. Behind him, horns blared as the Mercedes tried to match Jim's maneuver and failed. *Yes!* He made it.

He drove across the overpass and turned his car back toward Crawdad Beach.

Rats. He should have gotten the car's license plate so one of his police buddies could have found out who owned the vehicle. As it was now, he had no concrete proof to give law enforcement. However, the experience had given Jim an *excellent* idea for his story.

"With your language skills, you could volunteer on mission trips or join those groups who help others after a disaster, like a hurricane or tornado."

"True." Mia nodded at Stella's suggestion. "That's a possibility." Being in a group that did missions of mercy would be nice. Then again, she probably should avoid being photographed, and there always was the danger of running into someone who might know her. How could she stay active yet work behind the scenes?

"Will Valentino now be known as the Eliminator?"

Mia scrunched up her nose. Relinquishing her title would be best, but leaving behind her moniker still stung. "We'll discuss the details when I meet him this afternoon." Mia stood. "I better be going."

Stella rose next to her. "Are you stepping away because of what you swore when Andreas was killed?"

Mia groaned at the name of the man she'd loved. Just hearing Andreas's name again made her heart squeeze in pain.

"I'm sorry. I shouldn't have said anything." Stella laid a gentle hand on Mia's arm.

"No, it's okay. I take that back. It's *not* okay." Mia swiped away a tear. She hated crying. "Why does it still hurt so much after all these years?"

"You loved him, and he loved you."

Mia turned away. "I'll talk to you later." Before Stella could say anything else, Mia ran toward her house. She'd lost the man she loved, and now she'd relinquished her business. What was left for her?

She turned the street corner and kept going. She didn't doubt Valentino would make her proud. He repeatedly showed he was trustworthy and excelled on every mission. Criminals had been brought to justice and people rescued. He'd even saved her life a few times. Nearing her house, she slowed her pace.

Valentino, with a serious expression, stood on her front porch waiting.

Mia used her phone to turn off the alarm, unlocked the door, and motioned for him to follow. "Am I late?"

"No, but we need to talk."

"What's on your mind?" She sat on the couch as he settled in the wingback chair across from her.

Valentino scrubbed a hand across his face. "It feels wrong. You know other people who could step into your shoes much better than me."

"I'm not sure about that. I think you're the man for the job. My decision may seem sudden, but it was time."

"But, people trust you. You have decades of experience."

"That's part of the problem," Mia said. The years are

starting to take their toll. I'll be honest, this isn't easy. I don't know what's next, but it's time. I'll be available to help answer any questions and provide support. But now it's up to you to build your team."

"I always pictured a slower process," Valentino said. "You showing me the ropes for years or at least several months before you stepped away."

"That's what I've been doing all along. You have every skill you need for any job you decide to handle. Remember, you don't have to take every request that comes your way. Pray and ask God for guidance."

Valentino surveyed her for a moment. "Is that why you were always successful?"

"I wish all my missions had ended perfectly, but they didn't. Prayer wasn't on my agenda at first." She would always regret the time she hadn't prayed. "Be careful what projects you take and who you allow to accompany you. Get as much intel as possible. And pray. I should have done much more of that over the years. Prayer doesn't guarantee succcss, but without God's covering and guidance, you might as well stay locked in your room."

Valentino rose to his feet. "Thank you for believing in me."

"Please promise me you'll pray before you take any assignment and never ignore the feeling that something isn't right." Mia walked him to the door.

"I promise."

Mia laid her fingers on his arm. "One more thing. Talk to

your parents and get their guidance and blessing. They're good people who love God. If they tell you to step away, please do so."

"Okay." He gave her a quick nod. "I'll call them when I get to the hotel."

Mia hugged Valentino tight and then closed the door behind him. She'd worked the last thirty years trying to atone for her mistakes. It would never be enough.

Sinking to her knees, Mia sobbed.

Chapter 12

She hated to cry. It was so disgustingly emotional. Mia boxed up her files to give to Valentino. After she finished, she crossed to the shelves on her office wall and tugged on the copy of *War and Peace*. The bookcase swung open, revealing her very impressive weapon stash. She loved this hidden room and what it contained. Her friend Stella had the door installed when she first bought the house, and since Mia now owned the home, the room belonged to her.

What should she do with her prized possessions? Mia sighed. Her weapons had been with her for years, protecting and keeping her safe. How could she part with any of them?

Next time Valentino came over, she'd see what he needed. The rest she'd keep for now—especially her favorite tasers. Mia chuckled at the memory of the two guys last year who tried to harm Stella. Mia had given them both a nice jolt of reality.

She closed the bookcase and ran her hand through her hair. What could she do now? Yardwork? Cooking? Cleaning? Vacuuming? Mia stifled a frustrated scream. She wasn't cut out to be a domestic woman. Not that anything was wrong with that, but not for her. She needed to rescue someone and remove evil from the world.

If she didn't stay in motion, she would wither and die. Mia grabbed her cell and sent Valentino a message. She would make changes, but there was no way she could go with full retirement.

Seventy-five pages. Detective Larson was on a roll. Jim mentally patted himself on the back. This was his most productive writing day ever. His manuscript finally flowed free with mystery, suspense, faith, and a touch of romance.

Between the information he'd gathered earlier from Mia and his personal experience in a car chase, this had to be his best work. Jim saved his file on the computer, backed it up to a separate drive, and then sent the latest to his writing buddy for critique. Even though his friend's primary genre was Westerns, they exchanged chapters and kept one another motivated, making the writing process more enjoyable.

Jim's stomach rumbled, and he checked the time. Good grief. It was almost two in the afternoon, and he hadn't eaten breakfast or lunch. Since he was at a good stopping point in his manuscript, he'd grab a bite at Tiddlywinks, then stretch his legs with a stroll around downtown.

He locked up his apartment, trotted down the stairs, and stepped out onto the Main Street sidewalk. The day was perfect—plenty of sunshine, warm but not hot, with a slight breeze. For a Thursday afternoon, the little town was surprisingly busy.

Two young women pushing strollers greeted him as they passed by. A group of older women chatted as they made their way inside Knick Knacks Antique Store.

A silver-haired older gentleman, walking a little black and white dog, stopped in front of him. "You must be Jim Petterson." His blue eyes radiated a welcoming joy.

"Yes, sir." Jim shook the man's outstretched hand.

"I'm Henry Doss." He pointed to his little dog standing next to him. "This is Filbert." The dog wagged and even seemed to smile. "Chester told me you had moved here," Henry continued. "Welcome to Crawdad Beach. I hope you've found the town friendly and welcoming."

"Nice to meet you, Henry and Filbert. And yes, everyone has been great."

"Good. I'm pleased to hear that. If you're looking for a church home, we'd love to have you visit. I'm sure you passed the white-steepled church as you came here."

"Yes, I did notice the building. And, sure, I'd love to come." Jim didn't mind the invitation. He needed to put down roots, and attending church would be a great place to keep his focus on God and connect with the townspeople.

"Excellent. Come early." Smelling of soap and sunshine, Henry leaned closer as though sharing a secret. "We have donuts and coffee in the lobby before the service."

"That sounds even better. Thanks."

Henry smiled. "Well, I hope you have a pleasant afternoon."

"Thank you. You, too." Jim grinned as the man and his

dog strolled away.

Jim walked to Tiddlywinks, entered the restaurant, and chose a table by the big window at the front so he could people-watch.

A cute, blonde waitress took his order, and Jim glanced around the restaurant. Most people must have already finished lunch since there weren't many customers.

Jim did notice Valentino sitting at a back table, talking with a brunette waitress. From the look on their faces, they were both infatuated with one another. Jim turned away. He'd been in love before, and that did not turn out well.

Since his divorce, he'd dated a few times. He'd been serious about one woman until he saw her online dating profile filled with comments from the many men she was dating at the same time as him.

The waitress brought his food, and Jim tried redirecting his thoughts. He had a manuscript to finish. He'd left Detective Larson in his office at the precinct, reviewing files. Jim chewed his food as he considered his story. Some authors plotted their manuscripts from start to finish. Others, like himself, were known as seat-of-the-pants writers. Jim had an idea of how he wanted the book to end but had no clue what would happen in between.

He enjoyed the writing process, especially when something unexpected happened. His favorite scene in one of his best-selling novels came as he wrote, and an unexpected character entered the story. Jim rubbed his arm where chill bumps appeared. Some people might think he was crazy, but his imaginary characters did seem to have a mind of their own.

After a great meal, Jim headed back to his apartment. As he walked down the sidewalk, he stopped. A black Mercedes C-Class was parked across the street. The way the sun hit the car, Jim could see the outline of someone sitting in the driver's seat through the tinted windows. Was that the same car that followed him?

Not wanting to return to his apartment, Jim acted casual as he walked toward the antique store. Maybe the owners would let him go out the back of their store.

A little bell over the door dinged as he entered.

"Welcome to Knick Knacks, Jim Petterson." Grinning, Chester Taylor stood behind the counter.

"What are you doing here?" Jim walked toward him.

"I help out Jeremy and Grace when they want a day off or need to run an errand."

"I'm glad to see you. I need advice."

"Sure. How can I help?"

Jim motioned with his chin toward the front window. "I'm being followed by a guy in a black Mercedes."

Chester snorted a chuckle. "You're a mystery writer. Of course, you imagine you're being followed."

"It is not my imagination. The same car tailed me when I went to the beach the other day. He's sitting across the street right now."

Chester's gaze turned serious as he removed his cell phone from his back jeans pocket. "I'll call the police. Chief or Gabriel can get here in a hurry."

While he waited, Jim surveyed the store. The old building was crowded with antique and repurposed furniture, glassware, antique jewelry, art, old toys, and what would be considered knick-knacks.

"Chief is on his way," Chester said as he returned his cell to his pocket. "So, who do you think is tailing you?"

"I don't have any idea. It's not like I've led an exciting life outside my novels."

Chester rubbed his chin. "Could it be your ex-wife's lover? Girlfriend's brother? Bill collector? IRS guy?" He snapped his fingers. "I've got it. Don't you sometimes use actual cold cases to base some of your stories?"

"Yes, but I change names, locations, and the timeframe of the crimes I use."

"What if your Detective Larson solved one of the cases, and the true-life criminal is worried he will be discovered?"

Jim's stomach dropped. "That's a disturbing thought."

Chester shrugged as he walked to the front of the store. "Only thing I can think of." He adjusted a lamp on an old desk and glanced out the window.

"If what you're thinking is true, why would someone tail me because a crime was solved in a novel?" Jim moved behind a dresser where he could watch and not be seen. "Wouldn't that person want to stay anonymous? Why put themselves at risk of being discovered?"

"Good point. Since I'm not a criminal, I wouldn't know. Maybe the Chief will have an idea when he gets here. But your car just left."

Jim groaned. Sure enough, the Mercedes was no longer there. "I can't believe it. I should have gotten the license plate."

"You sure should have," Chester said as he texted someone. "Lucky for you, you have an intelligent friend."

"You got the license number?"

"Yep. Just sent it to Chief Weaver. You know, since someone seems to be actually following you, I think you should hire Mia as your bodyguard." Chester grinned.

"Hire her? That's not happening. I can take care of myself." At least, he hoped so. Being around Mia would be nice, but he was a mystery writer. Detective Larson and he could take care of any difficulties that might arise.

"Have you ever been in this kind of situation?"

"Well, no." Jim crossed his arms. "But, I'll be careful."

Chester tskd. "Besides studying and writing about the criminal element, I assume you haven't dealt directly with them. Therefore, hiring Mia is your best option. Don't worry. I'll take care of everything for you." He took his cell phone out of his pocket and walked away.

Chapter 13

Ignoring the incoming call on her phone, Mia pushed the box containing her files across the desk toward Valentino. "Go through and see what you want to keep. You can take the files with you, or I can have them delivered through a secure service."

"I didn't think you could do it." He grinned her way. "I knew the great Eliminator could never retire."

"No, I *am* retiring from being the team leader. You are now in charge, but you're stuck with me until I kick the bucket."

"I don't see that happening." Humor sparked in his dark eyes. "No bucket would survive your kick."

Mia chuckled as she crossed to her bookcase and opened her secret room. "Take what you'd like."

Wide-eyed, Valentino whistled as he stepped next to her. "I am impressed."

"I do like to be prepared."

"Are you serious?" He ran his hand along the weapons. "You will let me take some of these?"

"If you're going to do the job, you better be ready. Have you decided where you'll make your home base?"

Valentino averted his gaze as he placed his hands in his

back jeans pocket. "I am not sure anymore."

Mia hiked an eyebrow. "Your indecision wouldn't happen to have anything to do with a certain waitress, would it?"

"Perhaps." Valentino studied one of her weapons.

She wasn't often surprised, but his instant attraction to Ursula had caught her off guard. "Would you care to share what's happening with you two?"

"I have never known anyone like her."

"She is beautiful and seems nice."

"There is more." Valentino turned to Mia. "Something deeper. Outside is a beautiful woman, but inside is a beautiful soul." He thumped his chest.

Before her legs gave out, Mia moved to her desk and sank into her chair. She'd never heard anything so lovely. "But, you barely know her."

"True. I must explore." He stood before her, leaned forward, and placed his hands on her desk. "I will not rush. I will take my time with Ursula."

Mia studied him. "Are you up for taking on missions when you're thinking like this? Relationships in our line of business can bring serious complications." She knew all too well the danger of personal distractions and letting a heart beat with emotions.

"I am aware. I will be careful. I will not take any missions right now. Not today, no. And in the future, I will not take a job if I cannot work with excellence." Valentino straightened and grinned. "How about you? Care to explain about your situation?"

Mia feigned innocence. "What situation?"

Valentino shook his head as he picked up the box and moved to the door. "You not talking about Jim, doesn't mean the problem does not exist. You like him. Perhaps it's time for you to enjoy your life. I'll come back tomorrow to choose weapons."

After he left, Mia stared at the ceiling. Why didn't God have some skywriting for her? Tell her exactly what she should do. She thought she was supposed to retire but then balked and couldn't do it. She'd avoided Jim for weeks and yet still thought about him. She even dreamed about him last night.

Mia shoved out of her chair, walked to her front window, and stared outside. She missed feeling in control. Her skills had gotten her through situations most people could never handle. But this? Now? She had no regular life skills.

A black Mercedes slowly cruised past her house. She'd never seen that vehicle in town before, but it did look similar to what one of her old nemesis had driven. Mia grinned. Things just got a lot more interesting.

After reporting what happened to the Crawdad Beach police chief, Jim spent two hours searching through his files to see if one of his novels might have caused someone to follow him. Most cases he'd used for his stories had been over fifty years old—all but one.

Sixteen years ago, a nineteen-year-old college student went missing. The young man had left his dorm room one evening to go to a club but never returned. From all accounts, he was a likable kid, did well in school, and liked to party. The police surmised he'd hitched a ride with the wrong person.

Jim had written one of his novels using what he'd learned from case files and conversations with the police. He'd changed the location from North Carolina to Georgia, the young man's age and where he attended school. His Detective Larson had solved the case by arresting another college student who had been the missing young man's best friend.

His cell signaled an incoming call. Jim answered and listened as the Crawdad police officer, Gabriel, explained that the license plates on the Mercedes had been reported stolen six months before. Jim thanked the officer, disconnected the call, and leaned back in his chair. Whoever was driving the car was trying to cover their tracks. The driver's identity might not be known yet, but the stolen license plates would work well in one of his stories.

Maybe the person thought Jim's car belonged to someone else. There was no way his life was interesting enough to merit attention, much less for him to be in danger. Besides that, he was living in Crawdad Beach. Nothing interesting probably happened in this little town.

Jim returned his attention to his computer, where he left his story. Detective Larson was waiting, and he had a deadline to meet.

Chapter 14

Staring at herself in the mirror, Mia checked her look. She was wearing one of her more interesting disguises. A curly, mousy gray wig covered her hair, makeup had aged her face by thirty years, and her clothes and shoes were something she would not be caught dead in. Nobody would notice her now. Hunching her back, she took a cane and shuffled out the door.

Keeping watch for the Mercedes, Mia made her way downtown.

"Good morning!" Henry Doss greeted her as he came her way. "Can I be of assistance?" From the look on his face, he didn't know who she was.

"Thank you, but I'm fine." Mia wobbled her voice. "Just out for a stroll."

Henry slowed his pace and stayed beside her. "I'm Henry Doss. I haven't seen you before. Are you staying with friends and relatives or staying at our hotel?"

Mia fought an inward groan. She'd forgotten how friendly the people were, no matter the age or race of a person.

"Henry!" Chester waved as he crossed the street. He stopped beside them and matched her slow gait. "Who's your friend?"

Mia released a slow sigh. Her plan to stay unnoticed had

not worked. She stopped and scowled at Chester, "Would you gentlemen kindly leave me to my work."

Chester's smile vanished. He leaned toward her, and his eyes went wide. "Well, I'll be. What are you doing dressed like that?"

"I was attempting reconnaissance," she growled.

Henry and Chester leaned closer.

"What are you investigating?" Henry asked.

Mia pinched her eyes closed for a moment. Why had she thought her disguise would work? In normal circumstances, no one would notice her, but here? The Crawdadians were interested in anyone who came to their town.

She motioned with her hand for them to follow her to one of the benches along the sidewalk. With a groan, she lowered herself and bent over as though she could not straighten.

Both men sat beside her.

She kept her voice quiet. "I'm looking for a black car,"

"I know a man who works at a dealership over by the beach," Henry said.

"Are you talking about Sam Jones?" Chester asked his friend.

"Yes, he's a nice man." Henry nodded.

Mia thumped Chester with her cane. "I don't want to buy anything."

Chester rubbed his leg and gaped at her. He blinked a few times, then grinned. "Oh, I get it."

Confusion crossed Henry's face. "Could you explain,

please?"

"Must be a bad guy in town," Chester said.

Henry glanced around, then gazed her way. "Have you talked to Chief Weaver?"

"No, not yet," Mia said.

"What kind of black car are you looking for?" Chester asked.

"A black C-Class Mercedes."

Chester gawked at her, then chuckled. "Oh, this should be interesting."

Mia frowned at her amusing but often irritating friend. "What do you mean?"

"Nothing." He stood. "Come on, Henry. We've got something to do." Chester's mischievous grin slid her way. "We'll keep watch for the Mercedes."

The two men huddled together, talking, as they left her sitting on the bench.

With a frustrated groan, Mia got to her feet. It took all her strength to continue shuffling. She clicked her cane against the sidewalk as she made her way home.

What a ridiculous turn of events. She'd never been in a situation like this. Should she growl or bust out laughing?

She jerked to a stop when she spotted a black Mercedes turning into the alleyway behind Main Street. Why would he be going back there? What if it was someone new in town?

But wouldn't Chester have said something? Maybe that's why he chuckled. Perhaps the joke was on her. Oh, that thought made the blood in her veins turn into fire. She needed to talk to that man. Mia hurried her shuffle and turned the corner. Where had the car gone?

Growling, she made her way back to her house. She'd change into her regular clothes and try again later.

Writing was a blast when the words flowed. Otherwise, it was like trying to plow through granite. Jim paced beside his desk. His manuscript was coming together, but he couldn't figure out one of the angles he was working on with Detective Larson. The scene Jim wanted to write would end in disaster for his detective, and there was no way he would kill off his main character.

Jim grabbed his weights and did a set of arm curls. Getting blood pumping in his arms would hopefully get his thoughts moving forward. If nothing else, he was getting stronger.

He finished two sets and then checked the time. Eating dinner might do the trick. Feed his stomach and hopefully, his brain would kick in gear. Jim locked up and headed to the restaurant.

After a very satisfying meal, he stepped out onto the sidewalk. He enjoyed living here—friendly people, great food, close to the beach but not too close, and affordable living. Life couldn't get any better than this. Not ready to return to his apartment, Jim sat on one of the sidewalk benches. A young couple, holding hands, greeted Jim as they walked past.

He had loved his ex-wife, and she'd just walked away, taken his heart, money, furniture, and even their dog. In hindsight, he should have seen the signs before she left. The worst blow was when she admitted during the divorce proceedings she never loved him.

Jim shoved to his feet. At least Detective Larson had a love life, and he took satisfaction in ensuring every criminal woman was locked behind bars. Jim thrust a hand through his hair. He needed additional stress relief. A brisk walk along the trail might do the trick.

Chapter 15

She would not just sit at home. Determined to solve the mystery of the Mercedes, Mia walked the streets of Crawdad Beach.

At least now she didn't have to pretend to be an old lady. Ugh. She wasn't exactly getting younger herself. She swatted that disturbing thought out of her mind. Her granddad had been ninety when he passed, and he was active and a spitfire to his final breath.

Mia grinned at the memory. She hadn't thought about her grandfather in years. He was the one bright spot in her dark childhood days. The one man who loved her and taught her good things she would never forget. His faithful love for God made an impression on her that helped turn her life around. If only she'd listened to him when she was younger.

She turned the corner and stepped onto the downtown sidewalk. Spotting Jim about to cross the street, Mia paused. Should she talk to him? No, she'd been able to avoid him. Why change that now?

The sound of a car racing its engine drew her attention behind her on the street. The Mercedes was barreling down the road.

Running at full speed, Mia screamed at Jim. "Watch out!"

Why was someone screaming at him? And why was the Mercedes driving like that? Jim ran out of the street and plastered himself against a brick building. The car swiped within inches of his body and sped off.

"Are you okay?" Mia rushed toward him, her intense gaze searching him from head to toe.

"I'm fine." Surely, someone wouldn't have been trying to hit him. Either way, the incident would work nicely in his story.

"Get inside. Now!" She shoved him toward the door leading to his apartment.

"Yes, ma'am." He probably shouldn't grin, but wow. Seeing Mia in action was really cool. He inwardly groaned at his thoughts as he climbed the stairs to his apartment. He was a writer. Couldn't he come up with another thought other than really cool? When he wrote, he had time to think and ensure his words worked and were intelligent. Real life? Not so much.

Jim opened the door and stepped aside to let her enter. Good thing he had new furniture, and his place was clean.

Her gaze swept through the apartment, then to him. "Make sure you lock up."

Jim nodded. "I did."

Mia moved to his French doors and looked out of the blinds. Without saying a word, she crossed the room and checked his kitchen, inside his bedroom, bath, and office. "All clear."

"Thanks." He wasn't sure what to say since she stood there looking at him. He'd pay good money to see inside her thoughts. Then again, that might be dangerous. "Do you want something to drink? I have water or water."

"Are you not the least disturbed at what almost happened?"

"Oh, yeah. That was different." He couldn't wait to get that scene down on paper.

One of her eyebrow roses. "Different?"

Jim shoved his hands into his back pockets. "I mean, that wasn't good." Is that what he was supposed to say? He probably should be afraid, but going through something like that would be *great* for his writing. He tried not to smile.

"You are a strange one." Mia stepped closer, studying him.

He held up his hands as a nervous chuckle escaped. "I'm an author."

She released a puff of air. "So, you are. Maybe you're still in shock."

"Cool. I've never been in shock before." Another excellent opportunity for his writing. How did he feel? What were his thoughts after nearly being run over by a car? Should his skin feel clammy?

A sharp knock at his door made him jump. Okay, maybe he wasn't as in control as he thought. Hoping to act tough, Jim puffed out his chest and stood as tall as he could, fists ready for action. "Get behind me. I've got this."

"What are you talking about?" Mia pushed against him, shoving him out of her way. "I've got this."

Jim acted tougher than he was feeling. "This is my fight."

"Your fight? He's after me."

"Why would he be after you? The guy's been trailing me for weeks."

Mia's steely eyes narrowed. "You?"

"Yes, me." Jim tried not to act hurt. Guys weren't supposed to be sensitive. "I am a semi-famous author."

"True." A faint smile touched her mouth. "However, I've noticed the car cruising the streets several times outside my house."

"See, that's my point. The guy's been following me."

Mia released a breath. "Perhaps you better explain your thinking."

The knocking grew in intensity.

With a motion Jim didn't see coming, Mia sent him flying toward the couch. He collapsed on the sofa cushions with a thud.

"Stay there!" She commanded as she crossed to the door.

"Yes, ma'am," Jim nodded. Oh, man, he was so in love.

Mia pulled up the bottom of her pants leg, slid a knife out of a strap on her calf, and palmed the weapon behind her back as she answered his door.

Chief Weaver and the plain clothes policeman, Gabriel, stood in the doorway.

"May we come in?" the chief asked.

"Of course." In an amazingly fluid motion, Mia stepped behind the door, replaced her weapon, and acted like nothing was amiss.

The men walked to where Jim was sitting. "We heard there was an incident. Could you tell us what happened?"

"Sure," Jim said as he rose from the couch.

Mia stepped in front of him. "Perhaps I can be of assistance. I saw the entire event."

Sitting back on the sofa, Jim watched and listened, enjoying every moment as Mia gave details to the police. Maybe he could use his phone and film her as she talked. Probably not a good idea. She was such an amazing woman. Professional. Accurate. Observant. Beautiful.

"Mr. Petterson," the chief addressed him. "Do you have anything to add?"

Jim tried to focus. "No, sir. Not about today."

"We'll be on the lookout. Please let us know if you need us or notice anything else."

Mia let the officers out and then turned to him, her eyes blazing. "I am not a ma'am."

Trying not to say yes, ma'am, Jim sank back into the couch cushions. "Okay. I'm sorry. I meant no disrespect."

She steadied her expression. "Fine. Just so we are clear."

He gave her a quick nod. "Thanks for saving me. And seeing you with your knife was incredible. Can you do that thing again?"

"What thing?"

"You know. That thing where you threw me to the couch.

79

And this time, could you do it in slow motion?"

Mia leveled a glare at him. "Excuse me?"

"That maneuver you used would be great for Detective Larson."

Mia blew out a breath. "Your character?"

"Yes. I need to take notes." Jim hurried to his office and grabbed a pen and notepad.

When he returned, Mia stood with her arms crossed, looking at Jim like he was crazy.

Chapter 16

The man had to be certifiably crazy. Jim had almost been run over by a car and was completely unfazed. If anything, he seemed excited. Mia shook her head. She'd never met anyone like him.

Jim set his pad and pen on his coffee table. "Sorry, I shouldn't have asked."

Mia couldn't believe he wanted her to slow her movements and explain how she'd thrown him. Maybe she should give the guy a break. "Okay, I'll do it."

"Really?"

At his wide-eyed little boy expression, she wanted to laugh. Mia tried to maintain a neutral expression. "Come stand in front of me."

He hurried to her and stood there grinning. "Do I need to do anything?"

"Just relax."

Jim's shoulders wilted as he let out his air. "Like this?"

She couldn't help but smile. "Pay attention." Mia grabbed his shoulders and pulled him toward her as she turned around, tucking herself into the front of his body so they were both facing the same direction. Then she pulled his arm over her shoulder, lowered her body, thrust her hip against him, and

81

sent him flying to the couch.

"Awesome!" Jim flailed on the cushions momentarily before he could get to his feet. "Can we do it again, please?"

"How about I just tell you the steps so you can write it down?"

"What's the fun in that?"

"You're weird."

Jim shrugged. "Probably. But how will I learn if you don't show me? Can I try to take you down?"

She cracked her knuckles. "Just try it, writer boy."

Jim bounced like a boxer on his toes, dancing around her as he tried to formulate his moves. What was he thinking? She was a trained military specialist. What if she went on autopilot and karate-chopped him in the throat? Jim rubbed his neck. He'd seen that happen in the movies.

"You're stalling." Mia gazed at her fingernails as though utterly bored.

She wouldn't expect him now. Jim grabbed her shoulders, pulled her toward him, and kicked out his hip to catch her body.

The next thing he knew, he was on the floor, and Mia was sitting on his chest, grinning down at him. "You might be a good writer, but you're lousy at self-defense."

Jim tried to catch his breath. Hardwoods were much firmer than the couch.

Mia got up and pulled him to his feet. "Want to try again?"

There was no way he would back down from her challenge. Jim leaned toward her and glared. "I might be a slow starter, but I *will* be successful."

Mia scoffed out a breath. "Talk is cheap, writer boy."

Nice. He liked the nickname she'd given him, even though writer man would be better.

Best show her what he was made of. Jim made his boxer moves again, bouncing around her and waiting for the perfect moment. He needed this time to be faster, more fluid.

Like a tiger, he pounced.

Jim groaned. Mia had him pinned to the floor, his face smushed against the hardwoods as she sat on his back.

She leaned close to his ear. "Are you sure you want to keep trying?"

"Yes," he muttered. "Could you get off me, please?"

Mia chuckled as she helped him to his feet.

Jim grabbed her and perfectly maneuvered to send her body flying to the couch. "Yes!" He got in her face. "Got ya!"

When he regained consciousness, stars danced in his vision as he lay sprawled on the floor.

Mia sat on his chest again, glaring at him, but he could see a glint of mischievousness in her eyes. "Nobody beats me, writer boy."

He tried to catch his breath and get his brain working again. He had to prove to her he was more than a writer boy.

Mia got up and offered her hand. "Had enough yet?"

"Not even close." Jim vaulted up, caught her in his arms,

and drove her to the couch. This time, he was the one on top. He grinned down at Mia's surprised expression. "I am no mere writer boy. I am writer man."

"One couch take down proves nothing," Her eyebrow arched in challenge.

"Oh, yeah," Jim growled.

"Yeah," she chuckled.

He was winning. He'd got Mia to laugh. Man, she was gorgeous. He kissed her.

A gasp of surprise broke from her lips as she stared wide-eyed at him. "Did you kiss me?"

Not the reaction he had expected or hoped for. "Yes, I believe that was a kiss."

Her eyes narrowed into slits as she grabbed the front of his shirt.

Was she going to hit him? Expecting a blow to his face, he squeezed his eyes shut. Instead, Mia's warm lips met his, her kiss more gentle than he would have imagined.

Maybe he *was* imagining things. Surely, Mia Burns wouldn't kiss him. He opened one eye to peek. It was her, and she was in his arms, for real.

Not missing this opportunity, he kissed her again. She moaned, almost purred. He was no longer writer boy. He was writer man.

Chapter 17

"I need to go." Mia pushed away from Jim and hurried to the door. How could she have let herself kiss him? She'd been entirely out of control. She couldn't protect her heart if she engaged in lip locks with handsome, entertaining writers.

"You can't go now." Jim grabbed her arm and whirled her around to face him.

She stared at the looney man. "Why not?"

"You can't just kiss me and run away." He crossed his arms and looked like he'd been offended. "I'm not that kind of guy."

Mia puffed out a laugh. "You are a nut."

"I've been called worse." He grinned. "Please don't go. I'm sorry if I took advantage of the situation."

"You didn't take advantage of anything." No, she'd been very aware of what she was doing and thoroughly enjoyed his kisses.

"That's even better. So, tell me. Am I writer boy or writer *man?*" Jim shimmied his eyebrows.

Mia pinched her eyes closed. She'd created a monster. A very handsome monster. Before she could stop it, a grin took over her lips.

"I knew it! You liked the kisses."

Mia punched his chest. "Stop it."

His hand covered where she'd hit him as he staggered back. Now, his hurt looked real.

She grimaced. "I'm sorry. I didn't mean to hit you that hard."

"I'm a man. I can take it. But," he stepped closer, his hazel-eyed gaze searching hers. "Maybe a kiss would make it all better."

Although tempted, she held her ground. "We barely know one another. Maybe I'm not that kind of girl."

Jim tapped her forehead with his finger. "I think you're scared."

Her palm shot up, a warning glare in her eyes. Mia's gaze locked with Jim's, and behind the steel in her eyes, he glimpsed a vulnerability, a little girl looking for freedom. In a heartbeat, it was replaced with a stony expression.

Jim shook himself out of his thoughts. Surely, he was thinking like an author, not reality, because he couldn't see Mia ever being vulnerable. But, still, he wondered.

He took her hands in his. "Please don't leave like this. If you're uncomfortable being in my apartment, would you join me for a walk on the trail?"

She gazed at the floor, then shrugged. "Fine."

"Try to hide your excitement. It's not every day a semi-famous author invites a beautiful woman to walk with him."

That got a grin from her.

Late evening, shadows fell on the trail as they walked by the river. Mia hadn't said anything since they left his apartment, and he wasn't even sure what to say.

Jim looked skyward. He could use a good dose of heavenly help. Writing was much easier than trying to have real-life conversations. Spoken words couldn't be erased, backspaced, or rewritten; they hung in the air, often causing unintended consequences.

He stole a glance at Mia, her expression stiff, troubled. Why would she be bothered by a few kisses? Or did he really glimpse something inside her that she kept guarded? What was the gorgeous, tough woman walking beside him hiding?

A deep, low growl came from the bushes to their right. They both stopped as a pit bull walked toward them, the dog's tail up and stiff, his chest thrown out, both signs of a possible attack.

"I've got this," Jim whispered.

Mia crossed her arms. "Sure you do. I'll be here when you need me to patch you up."

He leveled his gaze on the dog, pointed to a tree, and yelled, "Squirrel!"

The dog stopped, his ears perked straight up, and with a loud bark, ran to the trees.

Jim did his best swagger move.

Mia laughed. Really laughed. He'd never heard a more delightful sound.

She held up her hand as though trying to stop herself. "I

thought for sure you were dog chow."

Jim feigned as if he'd been wounded. "You don't trust me? You know I've got mad skill moves."

"I'll agree with madness," she said with a sly grin.

The dog trotted back toward them, wagging his tail like they were best friends. Jim held out his hand to allow the dog to sniff. Since he wore a collar, hopefully, that meant he was somebody's pet. Jim patted the big dog on the head.

"Looks like you made a friend," Mia said.

"Saying the rodent word works wonders. Only the most hardened of the canine set are impervious." The dog grinned their way as he trotted beside them.

"I'll have to remember that next time I'm on a mission."

"I would love to hear anything you would be willing to share about your work."

"Not much to tell." Mia shrugged.

"Oh, come on." Jim panted like a dog. "Throw your writer man a bone."

She stopped. "Did you say throw?" Her comment came with a devious smile.

Jim held up his hands and backed away. "Just words, not throwing action, please. Unless," he stepped toward her and gazed at her lips. "Lip action is involved."

Grinning, she shook her head and continued on the trail. "You enjoy life far too much."

"What is life if not to enjoy God and what He has given? The Bible says in God's presence is fullness of joy, so focusing on Him, fulfilling His purpose in our lives, brings joy. Some people worry so much about their past or future that they can't see anything positive and miss what God is doing in the moment. And, right now, I'm enjoying the beautiful woman walking next to me."

"Flattery. Mere flattery." Mia waved a dismissive hand.

"It's not just flattery. It's truth. You are an amazing, beautiful woman, like a wonderful book filled with stories, adventures, mystery, and probably romance. But, that couldn't be as good a romance as I could write."

"You don't write romance."

Jim cocked an eyebrow. "I'm talking on a more personal level. We're just on page one of our story."

"You're assuming there's more?"

"I have no doubt." Jim sent her his best smile. "God wrote you into my story, and I plan on enjoying every moment He gives me with you."

Mia stopped and sat on a bench facing the river. "Jim, you don't even know me."

He slid next to her. "I'd like to."

She gazed at the river, then turned his way. "Mia isn't my real name.

"It isn't?" Proud that she was going to share something personal, he gave her a reassuring look.

"No. It's Hortense Hazelina Higginbottom."

Jim laughed. "You're kidding." When Mia's serious expression didn't change, he gulped. "I'm sorry I didn't mean to laugh," he muttered.

She stared at him long enough that sweat trickled down

his back. Then, she grinned.

"You were kidding me!" He nudged her with his shoulder.

"See, you don't know who you're dealing with."

He probably shouldn't ask, but he was curious. "*Is* Mia your real name?"

"No." Mia stood. "The pages of this story," She waved her hand between them. "Has to get much farther before that information can be discovered."

Mia thoroughly enjoyed Jim's goodnight kiss. She said goodbye, shut and locked up, then hurried out her back door to keep an eye on him as he walked home.

Staying in the night's shadows, Mia trailed Jim back to his apartment. He whistled as he strolled down the street, unaware of his surroundings. The man was either brave or clueless. She figured a touch of both.

Mia stifled a chuckle at the fun she had earlier as she showed Jim martial arts moves. And kissing him had been nice, *very* nice-way too nice to keep her heart safe. She sighed. What had she gotten herself into? How could she care so deeply for the man?

Jim turned the corner and continued until he reached his apartment building. Mia watched and waited until his light turned on. Knowing he was safely inside, maybe now she could get a good night's sleep.

His French doors overlooking the street opened. Jim

stepped onto his balcony, glanced around, and then stared in her direction. "I'm home safe," he shouted. "Sleep well, Mia!" With a laugh, he waved and returned inside.

Mia snapped her open mouth closed. How did he know she'd trailed him? And how could he even see her? She was standing in the dark.

Goose flesh raised on her arms. Had she underestimated Jim Petterson? Oh, she was in more trouble than she imagined.

What could be better than an entertaining, intelligent, great-kissing, faith-filled man?

Chapter 18

Mia ate breakfast as she thought about Jim's amazing kisses and their fun together. She'd barely slept last night. His comments about God had stuck with her. She was grateful for God's forgiveness, mercy, and salvation, but enjoy God and the life He'd given her? She was failing on both those points.

In a world filled with pain, heartache, and evil, enjoying life seemed wrong and insensitive. Yet throughout the Bible, joy was repeatedly mentioned. Jesus said He gave His believers His *full* joy. Even the fruit of the Spirit contained joy. Early Christians were beaten, abused, ran out of their homes, lost all their possessions, and yet continued to praise God, rejoice, and share the good news of Jesus Christ.

How did they count it all joy during trials and troubles? The Apostle Paul, who was beaten, stoned, driven out of towns, jailed, and shipwrecked several times, wrote about joy and rejoicing. Seriously? It didn't make sense.

Mia cleaned up her breakfast dishes. Thinking about joy shouldn't make her feel confused and guilty. When Jim talked about the subject, she felt like a load lifted off her shoulders. Maybe it was because of his excitement and peaceful, happy expression when he spoke. She needed to talk to Stella and stop thinking about Jim and joy and nonsense like that.

Mia put on her running shoes and headed to her friend's house. She'd talk about her retirement and avoid the other subjects.

Stella handed Mia a glass of lemonade and sat beside her in the deck chair. "You're traveling overseas with Valentino tomorrow? That does not sound like retirement to me."

Mia ignored her friend's pointed look as she accepted the cool drink. "I handed the business over, but I can continue to work. Just like you and Wilder still take on projects."

"When you said you'd retire, I thought you would step away from going on any missions." Her friend gazed at the sky, then slid her gaze back to Mia. "I think you're afraid to let go and trust God with whatever is next."

"Ouch. Don't hold back your opinion."

"We've known one another for years. I won't sugar-coat anything, and you wouldn't with me. If you felt God leading you to retire, *really* retire, you need to let it all go."

"You don't understand." Mia shoved out of her chair and leaned against Stella's deck railing. "How can I do that?"

"So, you won't let go unless you have something else lined up? Is that right?"

"Well, yeah. I need to stay busy. Keep going. Doing something."

"Saving the world?"

"Right!" Mia grimaced at her quick answer.

Stella leaned forward as she gazed at Mia. "What if God has something planned that you can't even imagine? What if

He's waiting for you to trust Him enough to release everything so He can give you something better?"

"But that's like jumping off a cliff without a parachute." Mia chugged her lemonade.

"Hardly the same thing. When you jump at God's prompting, He will catch you."

"What if I splat?" Mia tossed the ice cubes from her glass onto Stella's lawn and turned to her friend. "I've worked to support myself since I was twelve years old. I mowed grass, babysat, cleaned houses, cleaned toilets, and did whatever it took to bring a few dollars so my grandad and I could eat."

"I'm sorry. I knew you had a difficult background, but I didn't know that about you." Stella's gaze held compassion as she came beside her.

"Well, now you do. Other than my granddad, I had a rotten childhood. God made me to work. It's what I do and who I am. If I stop, it'll kill me."

"What if God asks you to step away so that you and Valentino *will* stay safe? Mia, maybe God is allowing you time to enjoy the life He's given you. And I've heard there's a handsome writer in town who would love to spend more time with you."

Mia blinked back at the warm sting of tears. She never deserved happiness or joy, not with her past.

Detective Larson was on the ride of his life. Jim sat at his computer and typed away. He had more ideas than his fingers could keep up with. Spending time with Mia had been incredible. He wasn't afraid when the car raced towards him because he was too busy watching Mia in action. Karate, jiu-jitsu, kung-foo fighting, or whatever it was called, had been the most fun he'd had in years. What a woman and what a kisser!

Jim chuckled, imagining the surprise on Mia's face when he said good night from his balcony. She underestimated his skills, and he planned on using that to his full advantage. Mia had a story, and he was determined to uncover as much as possible.

He continued writing but then glared at what he'd written. "No, no, no!" This was *not* the scene he'd planned. Detective Larson was supposed to talk to his client, not visit some woman—a beautiful, strong woman who was a great kisser.

Jim put his head in his hands. Mia kept showing up in his story. He didn't just want her in his manuscript; he wanted her in his life. But how does one go about wooing a woman like Mia? Woman wooing. And what exactly was a woo? He chuckled, then moaned. *Great.* Now, he was sounding like an adolescent.

He needed to get outside, get fresh air, or visit the bakery and buy something sweet. A jolt of sugar might get his creative juices flowing. And if not, at least he'd have a great dessert.

Jim's mouth watered at the great smells as he stepped inside Rolling in the Dough Bakery. A mural of a cartoon crawdad wearing a teal apron, holding a rolling pin in one claw and an oven mitt in the other, greeted him from the back wall. An antique bicycle and a display cabinet of antique bakery tools decorated the other walls.

Jim stepped to the glass front display cases to check out what they offered. Cinnamon rolls, donuts, muffins, and a dessert item called a crawdad claw. That, he would have to try. A cute young woman with light brown hair and dark brown eyes took his order.

With the crawdad claw and coffee in hand, Jim made his way through the crowded bakery and settled at a table by the front window. As he ate, he watched people stroll by on the Main Street sidewalk. The little town stayed busy. Maybe his next book would be set in a place like this.

Jim's eyebrows rose as an older woman, wearing a neon pink velveteen jogging suit, drove a riding lawnmower past the bakery. What made it even crazier was that she was hunched over as if driving a race car. The people around him and on the sidewalk didn't seem concerned. A few even waved to the lady.

Jim's attention jerked to where a black Mercedes parked across the street. Should he call the police or Mia? Jim stared at the Mercedes. Calling Mia would be more enjoyable, but he didn't want to put her in danger. Or would she put the Mercedes driver in danger? Jim took out his cell and placed the call.

Chapter 19

She had to stay strong. Mia pushed herself to lift more weight and complete another set. She was scheduled to fly out with Valentino, but her gut told her not to go. No, it was more substantial than that. What if God asking her to retire wasn't punishment but protection? What if that was true? What if God had something entirely different for her?

Mia stood, wiped the sweat off her face, and threw the towel on her weight bench. Why was everything so confusing? Jim Petterson was another issue. How could she have such strong feelings for him? She'd spent most of her adulthood trying to eliminate other people's problems. Why couldn't she take care of her own problems?

She needed divine help. Mia stared at the ceiling. "God, please help me let go of the things you want me to let go of and cling only to you and what you want." The urgency to cancel plans with Valentino grew so strong Mia groaned and called him. She wouldn't go this time or in the future. She needed to take a leap of faith and let it go.

Valentino didn't seem surprised and was even excited for her. He'd already called a mutual friend of theirs to join him on the next mission.

Just like that, she had nothing.

Mia swallowed against the emotion rising in her throat. She was no longer the Eliminator. Who was she now?

After taking a shower, Mia dressed and stared out her front window. She could get more involved in the town's activities. Join a book club? Attend a Bible study at the local church? Mia snorted. Yeah, that would work. She imagined herself sitting with a group of church ladies as they shared about themselves. What would she say? She didn't even use her real name and couldn't tell them anything about the business she'd been in or what she'd done in the past. Making up a story about herself wouldn't work either because she'd tell a lie in church—definitely not something she'd want to do.

She wasn't talented at cooking, so working at the bakery or restaurant was out of the question. Maybelline worked at the library, and Chester often helped Jeremy repurpose items for Knick Knacks Antique store. Stella and Wilder might let her help with some of their projects.

Mia sighed. She wasn't a domestic, town-type woman. Besides her elimination talents, she was a world traveler and could speak five languages. She stared at the ceiling and whined a groan. "Why? What am I supposed to do now?"

Jim kept aware of his surroundings as he walked to his apartment. Since no one had been inside the Mercedes, the police promised to keep watch for the driver.

He gave a slight nod to Gabriel, the plain clothes policeman, leaning against a light pole. Jim hurried up the stairs to his apartment. He'd left Mia a message, but she never returned his call. Maybe she was on another mission. Even Chester hadn't answered his phone.

Jim unlocked his door and stepped inside. Strange. He thought he'd left the blinds open. A crash shook his skull, sending pain ricocheting through his head. His vision blurred as he crumpled to the floor.

Groaning, Jim rubbed the back of his head where a knot was already forming and struggled to sit up.

"You shouldn't have told them," A male voice growled.

His head throbbing, Jim tried to focus on the man standing over him. "Told who, what?"

A stocky guy in his late thirties or early forties held a short-barrel revolver in his shaky right hand. "You shouldn't have told the world what I did."

Jim blinked, trying to clear his vision, and sent up a prayer for help. "I don't believe we've met before, so how could I tell anyone anything about you?"

"I'm not stupid," the man spat. "I read your book."

"My book?" Jim rubbed his head. He'd gotten some bad reviews before, but nothing like this.

"You wrote about what I did." The man pointed the gun at Jim's head. "I didn't mean to kill him. It was an accident. He was my friend. I never wanted him dead."

Jim rifled through his foggy brain on the topics he'd written about. His thoughts jelled. Was the guy talking about the nineteen-year-old college student who went missing? In Jim's book, Detective Larson surmised it had been the young man's best friend.

Hoping not to irritate the man, Jim gave him a clueless expression. "I write fiction. My stories aren't real. Detective Larson is a figment of my imagination."

From his back pocket, Jim's cell signaled an incoming call.

"Don't answer that!" The man jammed the gun against Jim's temple. "Get up! You have to write and fix this."

Jim gingerly got to his feet. "Write?"

"Yes!" The gun shoved into his back. "Go to your computer and write a retraction. Tell them it was a mistake. You and that Larson guy screwed up. It was someone else who killed my friend."

"Okay." Jim held up his hands as he walked to his office. "I'll write whatever you want me to write." Jim sat at his desk, turned on his computer, and opened a blank document. He took deep breaths to stay calm and placed his fingers on the keyboard. He'd have to remember how he was feeling to use in his next manuscript.

"Type this." The man shoved a piece of paper in his face.

Jim stared at the typewritten note. "You already have it written. What do you want me to do?" A blow to the side of his head silenced him.

"Type it in and post it on your website and social media pages," the man's voice seethed. "Every single one of them. I want it blasted for all the world to see that you messed up."

Jim tried to ignore his aching head. Did the guy not understand what fiction meant? He typed the man's rambling information into a Word document. Once finished, he signed the document Jim Petersen purposely misspelling his last name.

A knock on his door made the man jump. Maybe Chester or Mia had arrived.

The guy jammed the gun into Jim's neck. "Sit still. Whoever it is will go away." He stared over Jim's shoulder, his lips moving as he read the document. "Good. Now, open up your website and share it all over the internet."

Jim complied. Once it was posted, he cringed as it blasted to his social media pages. The note wasn't even well-written. How embarrassing. His agent, editor, and publisher would not be pleased, and his readers would think he'd lost his mind.

"Now the world knows you didn't get your story right."

"Okay. What happens now?"

The man's deep-throated chuckle made the hair on Jim's neck stand at attention. "Since you're devastated that you made such a horrible mistake, you have no option but to take your own life."

Chapter 20

"Take the pen in your hand," the man spoke slowly as though Jim didn't understand. "And write this." He handed him another typewritten note.

Jim read the message. He would never write something like that, and he sure didn't plan on meeting his Maker at this point in his life. Hoping to extend the time, he wrote as slowly as possible.

"Hurry up!" The man poked him with the gun barrel.

"I can't write with that thing in my neck," Jim grumbled. Unfortunately, his voice wobbled. At least he had tried to sound tough.

"Fine." The man pulled the gun away. "Just get it done."

A bright light flashed. The man screamed as he fell to the floor, his body flailing.

Taser in hand, Mia grinned at Jim as she kicked the man's revolver out of the way. "Miss me?"

He'd never seen a more beautiful sight. "Yes, I did!"

Chester and Gabriel ran into the room and took charge of the groaning man.

Jim tried to stand, but his legs seemed to have lost their strength.

Mia came beside him and provided support. "Looks like

you had an exciting morning." She led him to the couch and sat beside him.

"Thanks for saving me." Jim smiled at his beautiful friend.

"My pleasure."

The man was now handcuffed and in Gabriel's firm grip. The officer stopped in front of them. "Chief is on his way to get your statement." He hauled the man out of the door.

"You writers sure do have interesting lives," Chester said with a grin. "Do you need anything? A drink of water? A therapist?"

Jim rubbed the back of his head. "I'm fine, thanks."

"You're not fine." Mia feather touched his face, then his head. "The side of your face is already starting to swell, and you might have a concussion."

That explained his throbbing headache.

"Looks like you're in good hands." Chester chuckled. "I'll leave you two alone." He closed the door behind him.

Jim glanced at Mia. "How did you know I needed help?"

She gave him a sly grin. "Just one of my many talents."

Mia kissed Jim, wanting and needing him to know how much she cared. What would she have done if she hadn't gotten here in time? What if she had gone with Valentino? Mia fisted Jim's hand in his shirt and brought him closer, kissing him with everything in her. Jim moaned. Well, she *had* heard she was a good kisser.

His moan didn't sound as pleasurable as she hoped. Mia pulled back.

Jim whimpered. "I'm sorry, the kiss was great, but my head is killing me."

"I'm so sorry."

"No, it's okay, his grin was slightly lopsided. "Take advantage of me anytime."

She rose from the couch. "Let me get you some water and something for your headache. Do you keep medicine in your kitchen or bathroom?"

"Thanks. Much appreciated. Meds are under my sink in the bathroom."

Mia mentally kicked herself for pouncing on the poor man when he was in pain. But, blast it all, she was falling for Jim. Surprisingly, she was okay with the emotions right now.

She brought him a pain reliever and a glass of water.

He took what she offered, popped the pill, chugged the drink, and then, with a groan, stretched out on the couch. "Thank you, Mia."

The sound of someone knocking sent Mia hurrying to the door.

The Chief stepped inside to take Jim's statement.

After the man left, Mia sat on the floor next to where Jim laid back on the couch.

He sighed as his eyes slid closed. "I think I love you."

Mia kissed him on the forehead. "I think I love you, too." She couldn't believe she'd actually said the word; just put it out there.

Jim's eyes flew open. "What did you say?"

She might as well keep going. "You heard me."

Jim's gaze gentled as his fingers touched her cheek. "Almost getting killed was worth hearing you say that."

"How about not getting in trouble again, okay?"

"Sounds good to me." He sat up and kissed her, long, slow, and sweet. "I have a proposition for you," He whispered in her ear.

Mia swallowed hard. She thought Jim wasn't that kind of guy. She should have known not to let her heart out of its protective shell.

"I want to hire you," he nibbled on her ear.

Pushing away, she gave him a disgusted look. "What kind of woman do you think I am?"

Jim blinked a few times as though trying to process. "No, not like that. I was thinking of hiring you as my content editor."

"I'm not an editor." Plus," she quirked an eyebrow. "You can't afford me."

He cocked his eyebrow right back at her. "I bet I can."

Even if he paid her, how could she help him? He wrote best-selling novels, and she had barely made it through school. Mia crossed her arms. "I don't know anything about writing."

"I'll write." Jim struggled to his feet. "You help with authenticity."

"I could be your bodyguard, but helping you with your books? That's way out of my comfort zone."

Jim pulled her into his arms. "Take a risk with me, Mia." He kissed the top of her head. "You said you loved me."

She nestled against him, listening to his heartbeat. "You said it first."

"I did, didn't I? Then, you owe me."

"Owe you?" Mia looked up at his smiling face. "For what?"

"I took the leap before you did, so now you have to leap into a new adventure with me."

Mia whimpered. She could handle clandestine missions, gun battles, car chases, and bringing evil people to justice, but stepping into a heart mission was an entirely different matter.

Chapter 21

"**I**'ve got to get this down while it's still fresh in my brain." Jim ignored his aching head as he hurried to his computer and sat at his desk.

"Get what down?" Mia followed. "You need to stay still and rest."

"I need to write what happened. And since I'm sitting, isn't that enough?" He opened a new document and readied his fingers on the keyboard. He needed to describe his emotions, feelings, and what he was thinking as he came to after being hit on the head, along with his thoughts as a gun was pointed at him. Then again, what he'd been thinking wasn't all that interesting. What would Detective Larson have thought? Even better, what would Mia have been thinking and doing if she had been attacked? Jim swiveled his chair around to face her. "I need your help."

Mia crossed her arms and glared at him.

Uh, oh. Did he do something wrong? Maybe he should be resting? Was she mad because he left her standing there after their kiss? Jim grimaced. "I screwed up, didn't I?"

She didn't say anything, but if he read her body language correctly, she was *not* happy.

He rose out of his chair and stood in front of her. "I'm

sorry. It's just when an idea comes to me, I have to act fast so I don't lose it."

Mia took a deep breath, and her exhale sounded like a growl. She did not uncross her arms, nor did the fire in her eyes dim.

Oh, man. He had *really* messed up. A few minutes after they declared their love for one another, he ran off to document his day. How was he supposed to fix this? "Can I kiss you again?"

She punched his chest. "When someone opens their heart to you, do *not* run off."

Jim rubbed where she'd hit him and swallowed to try to loosen his tightening throat. He was more afraid of Mia than when he had a gun pointed at his head. "I'm sorry. I meant what I said. I have fallen in love with you." He rubbed her arm.

"You don't know me." A sheen of unshed tears showed in her eyes.

"I'm a writer. I love exploring untold stories."

"This is a mistake." She shook her head, then her back stiffened, and she stepped closer. "How dare you."

"What did I do?" Jim could feel his eyebrows rise to his hairline. "I mean, I'm sorry." He had really hurt her. "Please forgive me. I don't have a good excuse. I've basically been on my own for ten years. I haven't dated much, and it's just been my stories and me. I'm sorry. Please can you show me how to fix this? I don't want my next book to be how to lose a woman you love in 10.5 seconds. Maybe I should have hired you as a love consultant," he mumbled. What an idiot. He'd been given the perfect romantic moment with the ideal woman, and instead, he ran off to type on his computer.

Mia glared at Jim. She'd *never* been in a situation like this before. Should she punch him again or kiss him until he screamed for her to stop? Maybe she could do both. She fisted her hands.

Jim's eyes went wide as he stepped back. "Please forgive me. Can we go back to the sofa? It was safer there."

Mia grabbed his arm, dragged him back into his den, and threw him on the couch.

He sat staring up at her. "Don't hurt me. I've had a hard day."

The man was crazy. She was in love with a lunatic. "Close your eyes."

Jim whimpered.

"Close them!"

He squeezed his eyes shut.

Mia stood watching as his eyes remained closed. He was handsome. Nice jawline, Good hair, and very kissable lips. Was it worth the risk to continue and see where the relationship led? Maybe. If he turned into a jerk, she could teach him a lesson or two.

She leaned down and kissed him on his forehead. "Don't open your eyes."

Jim whimpered again.

Mis kissed his cheek, the tip of his nose, his chin, then kissed his lips. His whimper turned into a deep moan. Oh, yes. Now she had him.

He leaned into her kiss, his hands capturing her, bringing her closer until she sat on his lap. He opened his eyes. "Does this mean I'm forgiven?"

"I'm not sure. We may have to discuss this further."

"If this is the kind of discussion you are referring to, I'm willing to discuss as long as you'd like."

Mia couldn't care less how late it was when their discussion ended. She'd never enjoyed kissing anyone as much as she did Jim. Their time together had been fun, sweet, and sexy, but never crossed a line. However, her lips probably looked like she had a Botox injection as plump as they felt.

He'd walked her home. At least this time, she didn't worry about him when he left to return to his place. Mercedes man would never again bother Jim or anyone else.

Tomorrow would be a new day, and she had no idea what it would bring.

Chapter 22

Jim disconnected the call with his ecstatic publisher. His book sales had gone through the roof.

Last night, after he walked Mia home, he had called his agent, editor, and publisher. All of them acknowledged they had read online what Jim's attacker made him write and wondered if he had lost his mind, was trying to pull a publicity stunt, or that his accounts had been hacked.

When Jim explained what happened, they all jumped on the opportunity to contact news agencies and blast across social media about him being held at gunpoint. They were somewhat concerned for his well-being. However, their excitement that he'd solved a cold case in writing his novel took priority.

He would never again want to experience having a gun aimed at his head, but it did give him great scenes for his next novel. He'd already written five chapters.

His latest writing project was based on another cold-case file from decades ago. A man had been shot late at night in a foreign embassy in New York. The government of that embassy claimed the man had broken into their building and accused the American government of espionage. The United States government denied they had knowledge of the man or had anything to do with the break-in.

What made the case even more interesting was that no records showed the man had ever existed. Yet, someone had paid for the body to be buried in a graveyard in Leesburg, Virginia, not far from Washington.

Jim surmised that the man *had* been a secret agent. According to old news articles and research into the incident, there were numerous rumors, but nothing was verified. What piqued his interest even more was that at the time of the break-in, there were rumors that an American agent was being held by that foreign government.

To make his story fictional, Jim changed the time frame of the incident, moved the location to Italy, and made the mystery man, now called Alexei, a government agent searching for information to help lead to where his friend was being held hostage.

In Jim's story, Alexei would be shot, but he would live and succeed in his mission by finding and rescuing his friend. Since the setting was in Italy, Valentino or Mia could provide details on the area. Her military knowledge would also bring authenticity and help his story come alive.

Jim checked the time and groaned. It was almost noon. He should have called her first thing this morning. Jim saved and backed up his story, ran to take a shower, shave, and get himself presentable. Hopefully, she would be willing to have lunch with him and, if he was lucky, get a few more of her amazing kisses.

Mia tried to tamp down her anger. She'd already worked out, gone for a run, mowed her grass, and still hadn't heard from Jim. She'd saved his handsome hide and had a mega-kissing session with him; shouldn't he have called her this morning? The least he could have done was send her a text.

Oh, she would not put up with this. Fuming, Mia locked up her place and marched down her street. They needed some ground rules, or she would place her heart right back in its steel box and throw away the key. She would not put up with being kissed so wonderfully and then ignored, and she would *not* waste her time with another man who used her.

Mia opened the door to Jim's building and took two stairs at a time until she reached his apartment. She banged on his door and waited. And waited and waited. Was he not even home? She could easily get inside, but as far as she knew, he wasn't in any danger anymore. Not from an attacker, but she was ready to do more than throw him on his sofa.

Growling, she pounded down the stairs and out onto the sidewalk. Where was Jim? The sound of a honking horn flipped her attention to the street. Who was being so annoying?

The car stopped beside the sidewalk, and Jim poked his head out of the open car window. "Hey, good looking, want to go for a ride?"

Mia took a deep breath to steady herself as she walked toward him. "I don't get in any cars with strange men."

"I may be strange, but I promise to show you a good time and buy you lunch."

Not ready to be pleasant to him, Mia slid into his car and buckled in. "I was wondering where you were."

"I'm sorry I didn't call this morning." Jim gave her an apologetic look as he drove down Main Street. "Time got away from me. I made phone calls and then wrote several chapters of my new story. I hope you'll let me draw on your experience."

"We'll see."

"I'll take that as a possible, probable yes." Jim's smile was hopeful.

"Probably." Mia wasn't ready to return his smile. Even if he was handsome and smelled like he had just gotten out of the shower. She did love a clean-smelling man.

"Chester told me about a great seafood place over by the beach. Is that okay? Do you like seafood?"

"Yes, on both."

"Are you mad at me?" When she didn't respond, he cringed. "I'm sorry. I should have called or texted or brought you flowers."

"That would have been nice."

"You like flowers?"

Mia kept her gaze focused out the front window. "They're okay."

"You're not going to make this easy for me, are you?"

"No, I'm not." Why was she so mad at him?

"I'm sorry. I guess I didn't take you as a super romantic

type."

Mia glared at him. "Why not?"

Jim held up his hand as though she might hit him. "Because you're tough and can kick my tail."

"True. But I'm a woman. I like romance."

"You are *definitely* a woman and an amazing kisser."

"So I've been told." Mia cringed when she said that. Didn't she have enough regrets in her past?

Jim's forehead wrinkled. "I know you've probably been with other men, but give me a break. I haven't been active on the dating scene and could use some grace here."

Now she really felt bad. "I'm sorry, Jim. I apologize for getting upset. We aren't officially dating or have any kind of agreement."

Jim merged his car on the freeway. "Apology accepted. And please forgive me for not contacting you sooner this morning."

He was definitely cute. "I forgive you."

"Good. So, ready for the next step?" He glanced her way. "Mia Burns, will you grant me the honor of officially dating you?"

She gave him a grin. "Yes, Jim Petterson, I accept your proposal."

Chapter 23

A seagull hovered above the ocean as a light breeze provided a pillow of air for the bird to glide on in the salty air.

Grateful they'd found a place away from most beachgoers, Mia grinned at Jim as they walked near the water's edge. "You didn't ask Chester any questions about the restaurant, did you?"

Jim rubbed the back of his neck. "No, I didn't. All he said was that they had great seafood. He did *not* tell me the wait staff wore pirate costumes."

Mia grinned. "The food was excellent, and the atmosphere very entertaining. I'm grateful the parrot on our waiter's shoulder was fake."

"In my defense, the bird looked and sounded real. I wouldn't have tried to give him a cracker otherwise."

Mia nudged him with her shoulder. "I thought it was cute."

A hermit crab, his shell on his back, scurried past their feet. Mia smiled.

"You like the beach?" Jim asked.

"Very much. I love the sounds of gentle ocean waves."

"I'm sorry I didn't bring us something to sit on."

She looked at her handsome friend, whom she was

officially dating. "No worries. I'm enjoying the walk."

"Good thing. Since I've been inside most of the time, my legs are on the light side. I'd rather not be seen in swim trunks."

Mia slid a smile his way. "Blinding white legs, huh?"

Jim nodded and grinned. "Yep. Hazards of a writer."

"Speaking of writing. You want to share what you're working on?"

"I'd love to. So, here's the basics." Jim's pace increased, his arms and hands motioning as he excitedly told her his ideas.

As he continued sharing, a horrible realization came to Mia. Jim was going to write about what happened all those years ago to the man she loved.

Jim was getting even more fired up as he told Mia what he was working on. He hadn't been this excited about a project in a long time. This story would probably be his best one yet. He stopped. Where was Mia?

He turned around and spotted her. He'd been so busy talking he hadn't even noticed she'd stopped following him.

Jim hurried to where she stood, arms crossed, facing the ocean. "Hey, sorry about that. I got too engrossed in my story."

She didn't answer. Just stared into the distance.

"Mia?"

Still not responding to him, a tear slid down her cheek. She was so happy and carefree earlier. What happened? Did he say something wrong?

Jim put his arm around her. "Can I help?"

Mia curled into him. Clinging to him, she moaned and then cried. Long, hard, wracking sobs.

He held her against his chest and prayed for help. He'd never had a woman cry in his arms before. When she quieted, Jim kissed the top of her head. "I'm sorry if I did something wrong."

She whimpered. "It's not you."

"Did somebody do something or say something?" Jim whipped his head around to check.

Mia took a shuddering breath. "We need to talk."

He'd heard that line before. The one a woman said before they left him in the dust.

She slid out of his embrace. "Walk with me."

Jim matched her slow pace.

"Your story..." Mia gulped back another sob as she continued to walk. "You based it on an actual event, didn't you?"

"Yes." He stared at her expression. *Oh, no.* What had he done?

"Andreas was..." Her lip trembled. "He's the man who was killed at the embassy. He was my fiancé."

Jim's stomach clenched. "Mia, I'm so sorry. I didn't think. I didn't know. I won't write it, okay?"

"No." She stopped, her gaze intense as she looked at him.

"Tell his story, but let me help you fill in the blanks."

Jim pulled her back into his arms and held her. "I am sorry, Mia. Please forgive me for opening your wound."

She shuddered back another cry. "Jim, Andreas was trying to find me. I was the agent being held hostage."

Chapter 24

Needing release, her memories came tumbling out. Safe in Jim's arms, Mia shared the story of the man she had loved.

She'd been taken prisoner by a group of mercenaries supported by the foreign government. A covert American team had searched their embassy for information about where she was being held. The man leading the team made mistakes, resulting in Andreas's death.

"I've forgiven the team leader, but still," Mia swallowed a sob. "Andreas died because of me. He was such a good man. He didn't deserve to die, especially not for me."

Jim squeezed her tighter. "No, it wasn't your fault. You didn't take his life. You would have done the same for him."

"Yes." Mia moaned. "But, if I could only go back in time, I'd change many things. I would have been more careful so that I hadn't been taken captive."

"We all have things we wish we could change in our past." Jim's words were soft and soothing. "Mia, did you love Andreas well?"

"Yes. As best I knew how." Mia trembled as she thought of the tender kisses he had given and their sweet time together.

"I'm sorry he died." Jim's hand rubbed Mia's back. "Please

don't keep punishing yourself for his death. You said you've forgiven the team leader. Please forgive yourself. God's grace-filled forgiveness is amazing."

Jim held Mia until the sun sank into the horizon. He'd hold her all night if she needed. He prayed for her comfort and prayed that he would be the friend and man to help her.

Mia sighed out a deep breath and stepped away from his embrace. "Thank you."

"You're welcome. I wish I could do more and fix everything."

She wiped her tears and gazed up at him. "You did more than you realize. I had never taken time to grieve Andreas's death. I blamed the team leader, and I blamed myself for so long. And, you're right, I haven't forgiven myself. I've repeatedly asked for God's forgiveness, but I don't deserve it. I keep punishing myself."

Jim rubbed her arm. "God's forgiven you, please forgive yourself."

"I don't know that I can." Her shoulders lowered like the weight of the world pressed against them.

How could he show her? Jim glanced around and spotted a lettered olive shell. The smooth, shiny, cylindrical-shaped shell with brown markings was still in one piece and sticking out of the sand. *Just what he needed.*

He thanked God for the gift, dug the shell out, and

washed it in the water. He waited until Mia's sad gaze met his. "I want you to do something for me."

Jim placed the shell in Mia's hands. "Let this symbolize the burden you are carrying because you haven't forgiven yourself. Now, picture Jesus Christ as the risen Lord who conquered sin and death, standing with his nail-scarred hands open, waiting for you to accept His freedom. Close your eyes."

When Mia did as he requested, Jim continued. "Ask God to release the chains of unforgiveness that have held you captive. Pray and let go of the anger, hurt, disappointment, and your unforgiveness against yourself. Once you finish, drop the shell, let it fall, and listen to the sound of your freedom as you release it into God's loving hands."

Her body trembling, Mia's face scrunched up as tears slid down her cheeks. A seagull screeched in the distance. The gentle waves lapped at their feet.

Jim prayed that Mia could release the burden she had carried for so long.

The shell dropped with a thud in the sand. Mia gasped, and her eyes opened. "I did it. I gave it to God."

A wave surged forward, dislodging the shell, drawing it back into the ocean.

A laugh shot out of Mia. "Oh, my goodness. I feel so free."

Wrapping his arms around her, he held her close. "God's freedom is wonderful. Mia, no one can take away your sweet memories of Andreas. Cherish them. It's okay to grieve his death, but don't get lost in grief. You're still here for a reason and a purpose."

Mia nestled in his arms. "I've stayed busy, but I haven't been living."

"You still have time." Jim kissed her forehead. "I can't love you like Andreas, but I want to love you well. And I would be very honored if you would love me."

"Thank you, Jim." She cupped his face in her hands and kissed him. "But, experiencing new love at our ages?"

"This can be the best yet. Neither of us are naïve, and we know how precious time can be. Let's get married."

"What?" Her eyes went wide, and she playfully punched his chest. "We're barely into the first steps of love."

"Even better." He took her hand and kissed her fingers. "What could be better than stepping into marital love while everything is new and exciting?"

"You barely know me."

"True, but I can't wait to discover more about you."

Mia gazed up at him like he was crazy. She seemed to do that quite often. "You have no idea what you might find out. I have things in my past that would make you run for cover."

"Probably so. But I'd love to sleep with you in my arms under that cover and wake up next to you. Marry me. I want you as my wife, content editor, travel guide, and lover. Share my life. Let's go to church together and travel the world together. Let's pray together and love one another as long as God gives us."

Mia coughed a laugh. "You have our story all written out, haven't you?"

"Are you impressed?" Jim stood taller. "I just made it up on the spot. Give me a few days, and I can go down on my knee, present you with a ring, and develop an even better dialogue to woo you to my side."

"Woo me?"

Jim shimmied his eyebrows. "It's a good word, don't you think?"

"I don't know. You have to answer a question first. I need to know if you can love someone."

"Love who?" He readied himself.

Mia leaned toward his ear and whispered a name.

Jim gave her a curious look. "Who is she?"

"That's my real name."

"No! Really? I've heard of her... I mean you. I thought she, I mean, you, had been killed."

She grinned. "The reports of my demise were highly exaggerated." Her hands fisted on his shirt, and she pulled him closer. "The rest, writer man, is an entirely different story."

Epilogue

"You look gorgeous in that dress."

Mia sent a sly grin to her smiling, tux-wearing, handsome husband. "You're looking mighty fine yourself." She held Jim's hand as they walked the red carpet for the movie premiere based on his latest best-selling novel. "I'm so proud of you."

Jim squeezed her hand. "Your expertise and experience took my writing to a sky-high level. And having you as my wife keeps me flying high, too."

They stopped and smiled for the photographers and reporters.

"I must admit," she whispered in his ear. "I am thoroughly enjoying myself. You're my favorite husband."

Jim cocked an eyebrow. "I'm your only husband."

"See what I mean. The first *and* the best."

Reporters yelled questions, and Jim answered each one without hesitation or difficulty.

She'd been hesitant at first to be seen by so many people, but she wanted to support her husband. And besides that, who would recognize her now?

Mia's smiling gaze swept through the crowd, pausing when she spotted Valentino. He gave her a grin and a slight nod.

Her life had changed in many ways; however, Mia had no doubt her adventures would continue until God called her home.

The End

Thank you for reading,

Mia Lets Go

Lisa Buffaloe

To the Reader

Thank you for taking the time to read *Mia Lets Go.* I hope you enjoyed the read as much as I did as I wrote this story. If Crawdad Beach existed, I'd be putting together tour buses to visit the little town.

Perhaps, like Mia, letting go and trusting God for your future and the issues in your past doesn't come easy. God is a trustworthy, guiding, loving, forgiving God who helps us on our journeys. He also helps us forgive others (including ourselves) as we have been forgiven.

The world is a difficult and sometimes crazy place. However, God is always good. He will never fail you or forsake you. Whatever has happened in your story, and whatever happens next, "Trust in the Lord with all your heart, and lean not on your own understanding; In all your ways acknowledge Him, and He shall direct your paths" (Proverbs 3:5-6, NKJV). And, "Wait on the Lord; be of good courage, and He shall strengthen your heart; Wait, I say, on the Lord!" (Psalm 27:14, NKJV).

And remember, "What no eye has seen, what no ear has heard, and what no human mind has conceived, the things God has prepared for those who love Him" (1 Corinthians 2:9, NIV).

Acknowledgments

Heavenly Father, thank you for the interesting, sometimes quirky, and entertaining characters you have blessed me to share. Thank you for the gift of writing that You have given. All glory and honor to You, Father. I love You!

Dennis, thank you for loving me. Thank You for your support and encouragement. I'm so grateful God wrote you into my story. I love you!

Patricia (Pacjac) Carroll, thank you for the critiques, feedback, and fun assistance you give. You are a blessing. Thank you.

Jack Foster, thank you again for your creative Crawdad drawings used throughout the Crawdad Beach Series. Please visit Jack at jackfosterart.com

JoAnn Durgin, thank you for creating the beautiful cover for Mia.

Readers, I am so very grateful for each of you. Thank you for taking the time to read *Mia Lets Go*. If you liked the novel, would you be so kind as to leave a positive review and tell your friends? Thank you!

About the Author

Lisa Buffaloe is a happily married mom, multi-published author, and speaker. Lisa enjoys spending time with God, Bible study, writing, hanging out with her sweet husband, and enjoying God's beautiful nature.

Please visit Lisa at https://lisabuffaloe.com

Books by Lisa

Fiction

Crawdad Beach Series
Visible, yet Hidden
Running to Grace
Crystal's Journey Home
A Baker's Heart
Stella's Heart Code
River Steps Free
Mia Lets Go

Hope and Grace Series
Nadia's Hope
Prodigal Nights
Writing Her Heart
The Discovery Chapter
Open Lens

The Masterpiece Beneath
The Fortune
Grace for the Char-Baked

Non-Fiction
Float by Faith

Heart and Soul Medication
Time with The Timeless One
The Forgotten Resting Place
Present in His Presence
We Were Meant for Paradise
One Lit Step: Devotions for your journey
The Unnamed Devotional
Flying on His Wings
Unfailing Treasures
No Wound Too Deep For The Deep Love of Christ
Living Joyfully Free Devotional (Volumes 1 & 2)

Thank you for reading,

Mia

Lets Go

Lisa Buffaloe

www.ingramcontent.com/pod-product-compliance
Lightning Source LLC
Chambersburg PA
CBHW070337130626
46556CB00007B/2909

* 9 7 8 1 9 5 7 7 1 5 3 5 3 *